IN L♥VE, IN PAIN

Stories of Love, Loss, Betrayal and What to do Next!!

Dr. Janice Hodges Moss

IN LOVE, IN PAIN: Stories of Love, Loss, Betrayal and What to do Next!

Printed in the United States of America

   1. Woman--Fiction. 2. Man-woman relationships--
Fiction. 3. Domestic fiction. 4. Short stories.
I. Title.

PS3613.O779715 2012   813'.6
                        QBI12-600011

Acknowledgements

To my mom, Mrs. Ludie Hodges, for the lessons and the example; I miss you every day. Thanks to my siblings: Ernstine, Johnnie, James, Nathaniel, Willie and Shirley who have loved me, supported me and encouraged me. Thanks for the love and especially the laughter.

A special thanks to the women who have trusted me with their stories. Your pain has not gone unnoticed. I am extremely grateful to the friends and family members who read these pages and encouraged me to continue. Thank you to Anita Bunkley for editing this work.

Blessings to you all.

Introduction

"A fool learns from his mistakes, but a wise man learns from the mistakes of others." - Unknown Source

In Love, In Pain: Stories of Love, Loss, Betrayal and What to do Next!!

examines how women behave in romantic relationships. The stories of *In Love, In Pain* are not designed to bash men; the book could have easily been written from a man's perspective, as they, too, are lulled into destructive relationships. The book is designed to show how a woman's behavior, especially her decisions regarding the men in her life, affects her life and all of her relationships. It focuses on how women respond to what they perceive as love and how much pain they are willing to endure in order to stay in relationships that may not be nourishing, supportive or fulfilling. The book does not give advice, it merely points out the consequences of various decisions.

Over the years, I have encountered many women, both personally and professionally, who have found themselves in relationship hell. Loving an abusive man, being married to a homosexual or bisexual man, living with a perpetual cheater, having a husband who refuses to work or discovering that a spouse had children "outside of the marriage", are only a few of the painful circumstances that many women experience daily. During the years I've spent counseling women in various capacities, these hurtful life experiences have presented themselves too often. Since these situations are embarrassing, women, too often, suffer in silence. I wrote these stories to provide a means of assistance for women to understand that they are not alone.

By using fiction as a therapeutic tool, *In Love, In Pain* blends fact and fiction, self-help and romance. *In Love, In Pain* is presented as a non-judgmental, self-help, counseling guide. The purpose is to present knowledge through other women's experiences in a "painless" forum that allows women to learn by the example of others. This process boldly bridges the gap between fact and fiction, entertainment and therapy. It also encourages women to analyze their own behavior patterns in relationships and decide to make changes or not. *In Love, In Pain* takes a candid and informed look at some of the unhealthy and sometimes self-destructive decisions that women make in relationships. The characters are flawed and likable, bruised and resilient. They are full of passion, pain, and personality. The reader will be able to relate to the characters and the situations in which they find themselves. These stories bring attention to the feelings, insights, and pains of normal women who are in love and in pain.

The stories of Dedra, Marva, Sherese, Caitlyn, and Yasmine are loosely based on situations presented by women I know as clients, friends, family, and neighbors and through personal experiences. Each woman in these stories had to make decisions about how she would pilot the course of her life and how she would determine when her love was overshadowed by her pain. Each story stops at a critical decision-making moment. The reader is then presented with a list of multiple-choice questions to consider. The readers' answers indicate in which direction the character goes and what decisions she makes. By answering the questions, the reader adopts one of three distinctly different endings. Each ending is thought provoking and reveals the consequences of the reader's decisions.

The decisions made for the woman in the story could potentially reflect real-life patterns of behavior. The readers' chosen course of action will serve as a therapeutic tool as they see where their decisions and actions ultimately lead each character and how those lessons apply to their lives. Their decisions will direct each character to either to make better decisions about their relationships, or continue their pain. Women often believe they are only hurting themselves, and do not realize the magnitude of their decisions or how some decision inflict grave emotional harm on their children, while creating dysfunctional family patterns that are often carried from generation to generation. With *In Love, In Pain* I want women who are in painful relationships, or with men who don't have their best interests at heart, to be able to see their situations through someone else's story and be able to identify the various endings they can produce in their lives.

The stories included in *In Love, In Pain* represent the lives of real women of all ages, races, and socio economic brackets.

What unites them, and all women, is their quest for love. Their stories are not unique, and most readers will be able to identify someone in their circle who has experienced something similar because the same scenarios play themselves out in the lives of thousands of women every day.

When I have presented similar stories in therapeutic situations, the patient could clearly diagnose the definitive issues, the clues each woman missed, and the probable outcome—even when they previously seemed unable to do so in their own lives. Examining a story gave each woman the tools she needed to help self-diagnose her specific issues and allow her to transfer any lessons learned to her personal relationships. This method proved to be extremely effective as a counseling and teaching tool, and it can be rewarding for women in all stage of their lives. These stories allowed them to learn through the mistakes of others without feeling "preached to," judged or marginalized. Through *In Love, In Pain*, most women can receive therapeutic benefits without the cost, time, or stigma that is sometimes associated with therapy.

Caitlyn

A powerful bolt of lightning, reminiscent of a UFO's arrival, filled Cathleen's bedroom right before the earsplitting explosion of thunder cut off the electricity and forced her upright in bed. She sat up, trying to shake the eerie feeling that came over her. It wasn't just the storm; all day, the familiar tingle down her spine had been warning her of something. She stumbled to her feet, trying to keep her balance as she tripped over shoes, free weights and other debris that had found temporary residence on her bedroom floor. Cathleen found matches and lit candles around her room, and then began to rummage around in the piles of clothing, books, and papers around the old house until she found her tarot cards, which were under her altar. The tingling sensation was becoming stronger; she could hardy shuffle. She looked at the cards laid out in a "T" formation and spoke a single word.

"Caitlyn."

Cathleen reached for the phone, but thought better of it. She had to get to her twin sister.

*****

The scent of the cucumber-melon bath fizz filled the air, while the steam floated around the room like a ghost sneaking up on its prey. The combination of fragrance and steam was intoxicating to Caitlyn and she breathed it in with a smile on her face. As she eased her body into the hot water, she could feel the wonderful scented bubbles pop as she sat down. After working a double shift at the hospital, this bath was exactly what she needed. The tiredness she'd felt earlier was beginning to leave as she soaked up the scent and cocooned herself in the water.

The emergency room was always busy, but it had been overly so today. It had been a constant drone of activity: asthma attacks, gunshot wounds, and victims of car accidents, and even a patient who'd caught his hand in a garbage disposal. The ambulances did double duty--arriving simultaneously, vying for first dibs on whose patient was more critical. It always happened that way on a full moon--or so it seemed. Caitlyn's mental wandering took her away from the hospital to the old farm road where she had liked to play as a child. She was about to touch the sky in her tree swing, when a persistent ring of her telephone broke into her mental wandering. She started to get out of the tub, then considered letting it ring, but there was something about a ringing phone that Caitlyn had never been able to resist. She thought she had missed the call but her urgent hello found an audience.

"Mrs. Montgomery?" a voice inquired.

"This is she."

"I'm sorry to disturb you, but this is Bea from KHW International. First of all, congratulations on the birth of your son, Kyle! We received a request to add him to your husband's insurance policy, but we need a copy of his birth certificate. Can you fax it to me, so I can take care of this right away?"

"I beg your pardon, but who are you?"

"This is Bea from KHW, your husband's company, and we have a request to have your son added to his insurance policy."

"There must be some kind of mistake. You must have the wrong set of Montgomery's."

"Are you Mrs. Mark Montgomery?"

"Yes, I am."

"I'm the Benefits Coordinator at KHW and Mark requested that we add Kyle to the family insurance policy. According to my files, he was born about two months ago. However, I need a copy of his birth certificate to add him to the policy."

"There must be some kind of mistake. Our only son is nineteen years old. His name is Jason and he is in his second year of college."

"I'm so sorry Mrs. Montgomery, there must be some kind of mistake. I'll investigate it and straighten it out."

"I'd appreciate that. Thank you very much."

"Again, I apologize for the mix-up. I'll get to the bottom of it. Have a good day."

Caitlyn tried to return to the bath, but the moment had lost its magic. The tiredness was gone and the rest had energized her.

"I guess I'll do my housework before Mark comes home for dinner," Caitlyn said aloud.

Caitlyn turned the radio up loud, and began dancing and singing her way through the housework, stopping periodically to use the broom or a spoon for a microphone, so her imaginary fans could hear her. Four hours later, she stepped back and looked at her clean house with pride. The laundry had been done, the kitchen cleaned, the house had been vacuumed, and dinner was on the stove. However, she felt as if she needed to keep moving. Sometimes it was hard for her to come down off the adrenaline high of the trauma center's emergency room. She decided to return Mark's mother's casserole dish.

Caitlyn arrived and was about to open the door to her mother-in-law's house, when the door flew open and a lovely young woman carrying a newborn in a carryall rushed out, nearly trampling Caitlyn. When she tried to apologize, the woman, who seemed nervous, did not reply.

"Mom, who was that woman with the baby? Is she a new neighbor?"

"No, she's an old friend of the family. I'll be right back," Mark's mother said, rushing to leave the room.

She returned to the den with a laundry basket full of clothes fresh out of the dryer and put the basket between them. "Why aren't you sleeping? Didn't you work a double last night?"

"Yes, I did. But for some reason, I have a lot of energy. I should go to bed, especially since I have another double in the morning." Caitlyn carried on small talk with Mark's mother until 'Oprah' came on. It was a re-run, so she decided to go home to finish dinner. When she arrived home, the garage door was going up and Mark was pulling in.

"Hey, honey how was your day?" Caitlyn said.

"Good and yours?"

"Good, I spent part of the afternoon with your mother. I got caught up on all her aches and pains and the aches and pains of her friends and neighbors. I'll give you a full report of the "Arthritis and Acid Reflux Review.""

"Poor thing." Laughing, he added, "Did I tell you about the ache in my knee? I think it's going to rain."

Caitlyn playfully whacked his butt with the newspaper she'd brought in from the yard.

"Oh, now, I have a butt ache, too."

They both laughed as they chatted about the day's happenings. Mark got a dinner tray, took it into the den, and placed it in front of the TV, and Caitlyn followed suit. Mark flipped through the channels and decided on Law and Order.

"Oh, I forgot to tell you. A lady named Bea called today and said she had gotten a request to add our son, Kyle, to your insurance policy."

Mark took a long sip of water. "Bea is old and crazy. I don't know why they don't make her retire."

"She didn't sound that old, but I knew she'd made a big mistake. No more babies here."

"That's the truth. Been there, done that."

*****

Caitlyn rolled into the hospital parking lot with seconds to spare before her six a.m. shift. She hoped it would be a light day, but with two ambulances parked outside, she knew there'd be plenty of work to do. The shift was non-stop and they were shorthanded, so she would have to work late again. When she finally got a break, Caitlyn called Mark.

"Honey, why don't you pick up something for dinner? I probably won't get off until seven or eight."

Caitlyn was surprised to hear a baby crying in the background.

"Whose baby is that?" she asked.

"I don't know, some lady's. I'm in the drug store," Mark replied.

Caitlyn arrived home to find Mark stretched out on the couch.

"Mark, I thought you were going to pick up dinner."

"Oh, honey, I forgot. I'll go get something as soon as the game goes off."

Caitlyn was irritated but too tired to argue. She just wanted to get some dinner and put her aching feet up. She needed gas in her car and did not want to make two stops, so she grabbed Mark's keys off the counter, planning to go to the Piccadilly Cafeteria and get dinner. While driving, she almost rear-ended the car in front of her when she noticed a baby's pacifier sitting on top of Mark's CD's.

"What the hell is going on?" Caitlyn said, barely above a whisper.

When she returned home and mentioned the pacifier to Mark, he said, "I bought it for one of my salesmen who is always whining about this, that or the other."

Caitlyn thought about Mark's explanation all night. There were just too many things that seemed odd. Her mind was going a mile a minute as Mark slept contentedly beside her. She knew who to call to get all the gossip.

Caitlyn was glad Harold answered the phone; she never would have gotten a word in edgewise if Robin had answered.

"Hey, brother-in-law. How are you? I hadn't heard from you two, so I thought I'd better make sure you all were still in the land of the living."

"Yeah, we're here, but we've been busy opening our new store on the Westside. It's been one thing after another," Harold said, while chewing on something crunchy.

"I hear that! It's been busy around here, too. The hospital has been a mad house. We've had two ER nurses quit in the last month and one is out on maternity leave."

Caitlyn knew that if she got Harold on a roll, he could talk forever, and he'd tell her everything he knew, except how much money he had.

"And how is Mark? Probably playing golf every day? We heard about his promotion," Harold said.

"Yeah, I'm so proud of him. He works so hard. Maybe now he can rest and delegate some of the work to someone else."

To Caitlyn, an awkward silence seemed to follow her remark, but Harold didn't seem to notice. He rattled on for several minutes as she tried to figure out how to ask him what she needed to know. She decided to just spit it out. Caitlyn took a deep breath and tried to put a smile in her voice as she interrupted him mid-sentence.

"Oh, Harold have you seen Kyle?"

There was a slight pause as he crunched loudly.

"Yes, I saw him last week for Mother's day. Mark brought him by."

The gasp that escaped from Caitlyn's throat gave Harold's brain enough time to catch up with his mouth. He was silent for a moment. He knew he'd spilled the beans. Caitlyn slid down the wall to the floor; she wasn't sure her feet could hold her. She put her head in her hands and didn't try to straighten the cord that had wrapped itself around her neck.

"Cate, are you there?" Harold asked after a few seconds of silence

"Yes, I'm here."

"Cate, how did you find out? Did Mark finally tell you?"

"No, Harold! He didn't tell me."

"Well, how did you find out?"

"I just found out from you."

"Oh my God, Cate, I thought you knew-- you asked me if I'd seen Kyle. I thought you must have known. Oh, my God, everybody is going to kill me."

"Who is everybody? Harold?"

Harold sounded as if he was going to cry. "The whole family—especially Mark and Robin."

"Calm down, Harold. Is Robin home?"

"No, she's shopping with the girls."

"Tell me what you know, and I promise I won't mention a word of this conversation."

"I told Mother Montgomery that someone needed to tell you, but she said we should all keep out of it. I didn't think I should since I'm an in-law, like you."

Caitlyn didn't know what she felt; the madness and sadness were vying for first place.

"So, how long have you known?"

"For the last eight or nine years."

Anger was in first place now. "Eight or nine years! This has been going on for that long?"

"Yes, Cate. I'm so sorry, maybe longer. I'm not sure."

Caitlyn tried to take a deep breath to calm herself.

"Everybody has known, for eight years, that my husband has been cheating?"

"I think Mother has known for longer than that. It started when Mark leased the house over on Scott from her. He wanted to get Theresa and the baby out of that apartment."

The wheels were running in her head when Caitlyn said, "Theresa and the baby, then there must be more than one child."

"Yes, there are two children. The oldest is a girl named Morgan and she is about ten or so. Maybe nine, I don't know. And the new baby is a little over a month or maybe two, I guess."

"And how often do you see them?"

"On holidays and birthdays, mostly. Mark brings them over in the mornings and they leave before you arrive. Sometimes, he brings Morgan to play with the girls."

"So, this isn't like a minor affair. This is a long-term relationship?"

"Yes, but I know Mark loves you. It's been hard for him to support both families. He has two houses and three children. I don't know how he does it."

"Does she know about me?"

"Yes, she does. Cate, she is a very nice person."

"A nice person?"

There was an edge to Caitlyn's voice that scared Harold.

"I'm sure she didn't mean to hurt you."

"Well, that makes me feel better, she didn't mean to hurt me," Caitlyn repeated sarcastically. "She just wanted to fuck my husband and have his babies."

Harold was silent. He didn't know what else to say. After a couple of seconds, Caitlyn began to speak again.

"What does Theresa do for a living?" she asked.

"She's an assistant principal at the elementary school in Bay City."

Suddenly, Harold's speech quickened. "Cate, Robyn and the girls are driving up, I have to go now."

After Harold hung up, Caitlyn sat listening to the dial tone for several minutes. She couldn't cry; she was too stunned and angry to cry. She thought about all the signs she had to have missed. How could she have been so blind to miss something like this?

"So, I've been playing the fool for over ten years, while my husband has another family, and everybody knows except me." Her anger nearly rose to its boiling point. Caitlyn said, "I should kill every last one of them, and see who's laughing then."

The drive to Carter's Gun Shop was quick. She always passed it on her way to the mall. Caitlyn didn't remember any of the scenery: the stop signs, traffic lights, what route she took or anything along the way. She wondered who was in control of her body because she sure was calm and collected. She noticed that the clerk had the most adorable southern drawl she had ever heard. He greeted her from across the counter, looking over the top of his half rim glasses.

"How do, Ma'am? What can I do you for?"

Caitlyn was taken by his polite demeanor.

"I'd like to purchase a gun. Maybe a .357 Magnum or something very powerful."

The Clerk glanced curiously at her. She'd seen all the TV shows wherein the victim was always shot with a .357, so she knew it must be what she needed.

"Ma'am that's a mighty big gun. You must have some big rats to use as target practice."

Caitlyn returned his smile and tried her best to imitate his drawl.

"However did you know? I've got some awful huge rats, and I want to kill them all."

The Clerk's smile turned to alarm. Caitlyn had put too much emphasis on the "kill."

He said, "Well ma'am, have you used a gun before?"

"No, but I'd love to use one now."

The Clerk was no longer smiling. "Well, let's start out with something smaller. A .357 can have an awfully big kick to it, especially if you're not used to handling a gun."

Caitlyn recognized his concern. "I think I'll enjoy the kick. I'll take the .357 or something larger with some of those hollow-point bullets."

In the emergency room, she'd seen the damage the hollow point bullets could inflict. The clerk tried again to interest her in something smaller, more suitable for a woman.

"Can you tell me what you're going to use the gun for? Target practice? Home Security?"

Without even a hint of a smile, Caitlyn replied, "Lots of rats and target practice."

The Clerk wasn't sure what to do. He looked at her a moment then opened the gun case, took out two guns, and placed a .357 magnum next to a .22 automatic.

He said, "Now ma'am, you can see this .357 is a big gun. The .22 is sleeker. It fits better in your hand and is easier to handle."

Caitlyn smiled. "I'll take the magnum and the bullets. Hollow point bullets."

"Okay, the .357 it is. Okay, ma'am. If you'll just fill out this application, I will process it and your gun will be available in about three days."

"Three days? Why three days? I want this gun right here, right now-- along with the bullets." She tapped her hand on the gun to emphasize her choice. The clerk pointed to a large cardboard sign on the counter and said, "Ma'am, it's the law. I have to process your application first."

Caitlyn read the sign and smiled her, I'm so darling smile.

While tossing her hair to the side, she said, "I'm sure there are exceptions. I'm not a criminal, and I don't have an arrest record. I'm just a little ole housewife trying to get some protection for myself when my husband is working late."

The clerk didn't buy it. "I'm sure you are ma'am, but the law is the law."

Caitlyn looked at the application, wondering if she should go cross-town and try to buy a gun off the streets. No. She wouldn't know where to go or who to ask. But, rage could not wait three days. She stuffed the application in her purse and headed to her car. She began to beat her fist against the steering wheel as the clerk looked out of the window at her. When he came outside and tapped on her car window, Caitlyn started the motor and drove off.

When she finally calmed down and pulled to a stop, she was sitting in front of the elementary school in Bay City. The May heat was no match for what she was feeling.

Caitlyn entered the building and went to the office. She smiled at the secretary and said, "I'd liked to see the assistant principal, please."

"Mrs. Montgomery is in a PTA meeting in the auditorium. She should be finished in about thirty, minutes if you want to wait."

Caitlyn said, "Oh, I'm just an old friend. I wanted to say hi, but I'll see her later."

As she was leaving, she noticed the auditorium sign. Caitlyn entered, walked down the aisle of the hot auditorium, and stepped onto the stage. She stopped next to the woman she had seen leaving her mother-in-law's house with the baby. The woman looked as if she were going to faint. There was no struggle when Caitlyn took the microphone from the woman's hand and faced the audience.

"I'm sorry to interrupt your PTA meeting, but I have something to tell all of you about Mrs. Montgomery. You see, she is not Mrs. Montgomery. I am. She is just the little bitch who has been fucking my husband and pretending to be his wife--even though he already has a wife. This BITCH has two illegitimate, bastard children with my husband. She is not qualified to be here in this school with DECENT people who are trying to set an example for their DECENT children. She is nothing more than a lying, husband-stealing whore."

Theresa tried to run off stage, but Caitlyn grabbed her by the back of her cheap Donna Karen knock-off navy suit jacket.

Holding her with one hand and the microphone in the other, Caitlyn continued. "Don't run now, bitch. You've been fucking my husband Mark Montgomery for years, now!" Caitlyn looked Theresa up and down for a brief moment. Her eyes stopped at the woman's hand. Turning to the audience, she said, "Look, she even has on wedding rings from a married man. I've been married to Mark Montgomery for twenty- three years. He sleeps in my bed every night and goes to his whore when I'm working."

The audience shuddered as they watched the scene unfold on stage, like a school play gone way wrong. The parents and teachers were looking from one to another with shocked expressions. Finally, the glue that had frozen the pretend Mrs. Montgomery in place broke, and she tried to snatch the microphone from Caitlyn's hand, but Caitlyn slapped her and made her stagger across the stage. One teacher ran to get security.

"I'd like to ask you, whatever the hell your name is, since we both know it's not Mrs. Montgomery …do you like fucking my husband as much as I do?"

The pretend Mrs. Montgomery was crying, but Caitlyn slapped her again and said, "Don't cry now, bitch. You weren't crying when you were fucking my husband and giving birth to bastard children."

The security guard walked onto the stage and wrestled the microphone away from Caitlyn.

"Miss, we are going to have to ask you to leave."

"No. Ask that husband stealing sack of shit to leave. She's the one who has been fucking my husband and pretending to be his wife, lying to these good people."

The two policemen walked in and tried to help the security officer remove Caitlyn, but she proved to be a worthy opponent. She was kicking and screaming and trying to bite the policemen as they carried her out of the auditorium. As she was leaving, she kept screaming, "Where's your marriage license, bitch? Tell these people who you really are."

The basement holding cell was cold and damp, even in the May heat, but Caitlyn didn't mind. The blood boiling in her veins was enough to keep her warm. Caitlyn planned gruesome crimes in her mind against her mother-in-law, her sister-in-law, the fake Mrs. Montgomery and especially Mark. Caitlyn had been in jail for four hours before Mark arrived to bail her out. Once she was released, she walked right past him, and took a cab back to the school where her car was parked. The school was peaceful; there were no signs of the day's activities because everyone was on the phone recounting the incident at the PTA meeting to their friends, family, store clerks or anyone who would listen. Caitlyn drove home in a semi-conscious daze. She rubbed the marks the handcuffs had made on her wrist. She thought, Three hours until I have to go to work. When she walked in the door, Mark was pacing the floor in the kitchen.

"Cate, what the hell has gotten into you?" he screamed.

Caitlyn fearlessly walked up to him, placed two fingers between his eyes, and said, "This is where I'm going to shoot you."

Mark took a step back and lowered his voice. "Cate, why did you do a thing like that?"

Caitlyn stepped closer to him with a look in her eyes that he had never seen.

"That's a fair question, she answered. But here's an even fairer question, why did you do a thing like that? Why did you lie to me, over and over again? Why did you have an affair with another woman for over ten years? Why did you come home to me and lie to me with every word and touch? If you wanted her, why didn't you divorce me and stay with her? Why did you do it, you greedy bastard? What's gotten into me? I should be asking you, 'Who did you get into?'"

Mark walked to the cabinet and got a bottle of Johnny Walker green label. "Cate, it just happened. I can't explain it, it just happened."

"Oh, it was an accident. You just fell and landed in another woman's vagina?"

"No, Cate. It wasn't like that."

Caitlyn sat down at the table across from him, taunting him with a wickedly sweet smile that was not in her eyes. "Then, praytel, how was it, then? I wouldn't want to get any of the details wrong. Why don't you let me in on how it 'just happened'? After living a lie for more than ten years, I deserve to know the truth, don't you think?"

Mark took a big gulp of his drink and began, "Theresa was . . ."

"Theresa. Why, isn't that a saintly and virginal name for a husband stealing whore?"

Mark swallowed hard. "She was a teacher. I met her when the company sent me to speak to her students on career day."

Caitlyn interrupted, "And you told them how to grow up and betray their wives and families."

Mark looked wounded. "Cate, I know you're hurt, but we have to handle this like adults."

"Like adults? The adult way to handle this was for you to tell me ten years ago that you didn't love me anymore. Ten years ago, the adult thing to do would have been to tell me you'd found a young cunt named Theresa and that you were going to leave."

Mark hung his head and Caitlyn continued. "Oh, you couldn't say it, then, and you can't say it now, can you? You lousy coward."

Mark reached for her hand. "Caitlyn I didn't stop loving you. You are my wife."

Caitlyn took his drink and threw it in his face. "Don't fucking lie to me, Mark. If you loved me, you wouldn't have humiliated me and lied to me. Besides, that bitch says she's your wife, too."

"Caitlyn, I wanted to do what was right. I loved you, but she was young and pregnant. Her dad put her out because she was pregnant and she doesn't believe in abortion."

"Well, isn't she the damned moral one? She doesn't believe in abortion, but she does believe in committing adultery and having bastard children."

"It wasn't like that, Cate. We didn't set out to have an affair. It just happened."

"Just happened, and you couldn't have stopped it. You must think I'm cuckoo for Cocoa Puffs! Be real. You say it was an accident. Let's see now. Let me ask you a question. Where did the two of you have sex for the first time?"

"At a hotel."

"On the way to the hotel, you couldn't have stopped and thought, THIS IS WRONG, I'm a married man?' Getting out of the car, you couldn't have stopped and thought 'This is wrong I'm married? Talking to the desk clerk, you couldn't have thought, 'I can't do this I'm married?' On the elevator, you couldn't have said, 'This might end up badly?' Unlocking the damned door, you couldn't have thought, 'This could potentially turn my life upside down?' Getting undressed, you couldn't have thought, 'I might get this girl pregnant or get a disease I might give to my wife?' With each question, Caitlyn's voice rose an octave. By the end of it all, Caitlyn was screaming at the top of her lungs, while tears streamed down her face.

"At no time did it cross your mind that what you were about to do was wrong? Wrong! WRONG! Of course it did. But you wanted to taste the forbidden fruit so you'd feel like a fucking gigolo."

"I know, now, I've hurt so many people. But I wasn't thinking," Mark said.

"Oh, you were thinking all right, but it was with your dick."

"Maybe I deserve that, but I didn't set out for this to happen. But since it's done now, I want to do the right thing."

Caitlyn stood up and started to clap her hands. "After ten years you want to do the right thing. I guess I'm supposed to be happy now?"

"No, you're not supposed to be happy, but you're supposed to give me credit for trying to do the right thing."

Caitlyn said, "Oh, now I see. I fully understand. The right thing is to have us both. And what credit do you think you deserve for that?"

"No, Cate, the right thing to do was for me to keep our wedding vows and honor my obligation to you. I made a big mistake, Cate."

"A mistake is something you make without prior knowledge of the consequences. You didn't make a mistake. You calculated and planned to betray me and our family because you wanted to put your dick in places where it didn't belong, and you're damned right! Those actions are going to prove to be the biggest mistakes of your fucking life."

"I'm sorry, I didn't mean to hurt you, and neither did Theresa."

"You mean you thought I'd feel good to find out my husband has two children and another woman who thinks she's his wife? Oh, Mark. You're right. I feel real good about the whole thing. This is the best gift ever."

"Cate, what can I say? What can I do?"

"There's not much you can say. Your ass should have been talking more than ten years ago. Tell me, Mark. Why does the saintly Theresa think she's Mrs. Montgomery?"

"She would have lost her job, having a baby and not being married. That would have been a bad example for the children."

"And a better example would be for a teacher to pretend she is married to a married man. I imagine living a life of fraud and deception is better than being an unwed mother. That is a great lesson for the children to learn."

Caitlyn looked at her husband more intently this time. "What were you looking for? More sex, better sex? What did you want? Where did I go wrong as your wife?"

"You didn't go wrong. You are the perfect wife and mother. That's why I don't want to lose you."

"If I were the perfect wife and mother, then why were you in another woman's bed?"

"Cate, I wish a million times a day that it had not happened. She liked my Career Day presentation and called me to tell me so. After that, she called and I helped her get a donation from the company for her class trip. She reminded me of you and I did something I instantly regretted. I felt bad then and I feel bad now. But, I couldn't turn my back on a girl who was having my child, so I got a little house for her and the baby, and she was going to pretend that we were married and, then, divorced so she wouldn't lose her job."

"Mark, I almost feel sorry for you," Caitlyn said, her voice suddenly very low. "But not quite. I know about temptation. Do you have any idea how many times I have been propositioned by good-looking doctors, residents and interns and even paramedics? Don't even mention the women! Sometimes, I was even tempted, but I'd think of what I could lose. I'd think about how hurt you would be. So, I enjoyed the flirt and I came home and gave you what belongs to you. But you couldn't give me the same courtesy."

Mark looked hurt. Caitlyn looked at him for a long minute. "And Mark, what makes this so bad is that you killed my feelings a little bit everyday for over ten years. You constantly went to someone else's bed, while I struggled to be faithful to you. I wanted to give you all my love and you were running around having the best of both worlds … a wife …on the eastside and a wannabe wife of the Westside."

Mark tried to touch her, but Caitlyn moved her hand away, saying, "I hope you know how much you hurt me. Today, I went to get a gun to kill you, your mother, your crazy ass sister, and the other Mrs. Montgomery. How do you feel about that? Your actions could have caused four people to die."

Before he could respond, Caitlyn went on, "I have to go to work and when I get home, you had better have decided what the fuck you're going to do to straighten this mess out."

Mark tried to hug her, but Caitlyn gave him a look that told him to back off.

*****

When Caitlyn got home twelve hours later, Mark was still sitting in the kitchen with the same clothes on, clutching an empty whiskey bottle. Caitlyn walked past him and began to make breakfast. She made all of Mark's favorites, but only enough for one.

"Tell me what you have decided to do. I'm sure there were some answers in that bottle."

Mark looked ten years older. "I love you, Caitlyn. I always have since I was fifteen years old, but I love Theresa, too. It might be hard, but maybe we can all find a way to live through this. She needs me, we have small children, and I love my children."

"Oh, I see. Your answer is to have your cake and eat it too."

"I love you and I want to die with you as my wife . . . "

"After a three day waiting period, that can be easily arranged."

"I love you and I don't want a divorce, but I am not willing to give Theresa up. At first there was a lot of resentment towards her, but watching her with the kids, she grew on me."

"Isn't that nice? You want me to accept it so we can all live like one big, happy family. Next, you'll want to move her and the little bastards in here too. I'm so sorry Mark, but I don't THINK so!"

"I can't turn my back on my children, I made them. They are a part of me just like Jason."

Caitlyn jumped to her feet. "Don't compare your bastards to Jason. Keep him out of it."

"They are bastards to you, but to me they are my children and I'd prefer you didn't speak of them that way."

"I would have preferred that you didn't fuck another woman and make bastard children in the first place, but that's beside the point. What the hell are you going to do about this, Mark?"

"I don't know, Cate. I love you both. I want you, but I want to be with my kids too."

"You expect me to go on like nothing has ever happened?"

"Maybe we can all go to some kind of therapy and find a way to live with it."

"Well, since you have another woman, do I get a chance to have another man, maybe some nice young one who can service me and Theresa?"

"I know I deserve your anger, but it's not helping. Can we talk like sensible adults?"

"Well, I needed the 'sensible talk' ten years ago."

Mark grabbed his jacket and said, "I have to go and take my daughter to school."

Caitlyn lay in her bed, looking at the place where her husband's body should have been. She listened for the sound of his soft snoring, which usually lulled her to sleep. But, there was only silence. No tears rose to meet her eyes, but the anger was getting out of control. She was pulled from the abyss by the ring of the phone.

Mark's mother, Marguerite, was on the line. She said, "How are you honey? I'm worried about you."

"Oh, that's nice. Were you also worried about me when you were lying, stabbing me in the back, and covering for my husband and his whore?"

Marguerite said, "Caitlyn don't speak to me that way."

"Why not? I no longer have any respect for you. You are a liar just like your son."

"Caitlyn, I love you just like you were my own daughter. What was I supposed to do?"

"Well, Marguerite, I really feel loved, thank you. And, you were supposed to encourage him to tell the truth. You were supposed to tell him, 'You are a married man, you don't bring other women to my house. I won't be a part of this.' That is what you were supposed to do."

"Cate, I did talk to him, and whether you like it or not, she has two of my grandchildren."

"Not."

Marguerite said, "Not what?"

"You said like it or not. And I chose not. I don't damn like it. I don't like it that you smiled in my face and stabbed me in my back. I treated you like you were my mother. I tried to do everything I could for you. I did things for you that your own daughter wouldn't do."

"Baby, I know you're hurt, and we're going to have to all get through this. But, what you did at the school was wrong. Everybody's talking about it. You know how fast news travels in small towns."

"Oh really, now? What I did was wrong? Was anything you did wrong? Was what that woman did with my husband wrong? Was my husband wrong for violating our marriage and having two children? No, of course not. Everybody else is right and I'm wrong. Well, I have one more thing to do wrong and that is to tell you to go to hell. Don't pass go, don't collect $200, just go straight to hell, Marguerite. And if you see me on the street, don't say anything to me because I might just shoot your ass."

"Honey, I know that's your hurt talking."

Caitlyn hung up the phone and thought about Mark. She wanted her husband back. The pillow still had his scent. She pulled it close and sunk her nose into it as if she were breathing him in.

Caitlyn said, "If that little tease thinks she's just going to waltz in here and take my husband, she has another thought coming."

Caitlyn was mentally and physically exhausted. She fell into a fitful sleep. Her mind was racing too much to stay asleep.

Mark wanted to avoid more drama with Caitlyn, so he parked down the block and waited for her to leave for work. He was struck with regret when he saw Caitlyn emerge from the house, wearing scrubs, her long ponytail swinging in the breeze as it had done when she'd played volleyball in high school. He loved her and even though he loved Theresa, too, what he felt for Caitlyn could never be replaced. He had loved her from the moment she smiled at him in study hall. He wondered how he'd make it without her in his life. He tried to control his emotions but the reality of what he'd done made him weep.

Caitlyn drove to the gun shop and dropped off her application for the gun permit. She thanked God that a different clerk helped her. When she returned home, she was shocked to see Mark's car in the driveway with the trunk open. It was filled with piles of clothes still on hangers.

"That motherfucker," she muttered. Caitlyn came in the door as Mark was carrying another armful of clothes and personal items to his car.

"Well, isn't this the coward's way out?"

"You told me to make a decision, and I have. I had to consider that Jason is grown, but Morgan and Kyle are small.

They need a father. Especially, now… since Theresa's been suspended from the school district. Thanks to you."

"She got fired because of her own lies and because she was fucking a married man."

"You didn't have to do that, you could have come to me."

"Oh, like you came to me. Mark, you don't leave your wife of twenty-three years for some fucking bimbo."

Mark interrupted, "Theresa is not a bimbo. She's a sweet, caring person."

"Yes, I forgot. Theresa, the sweet, husband stealing bimbo who lies about her identity and pretends to be married to a married man. Yeah, that is sweet and moral, too. I see why you two get along."

Mark walked around Caitlyn and headed to his car. He placed the items in his trunk, shut it, and backed out of the driveway, barely missing Mr. Johnson's old Chevy pick-up. Caitlyn could see Ms. Gilmore peeping through the blinds. She knew this would be on the grapevine within the hour. Caitlyn stumbled inside, locking the door behind her. She made it to her bed and fell face down in it. She wanted to cry, but the tears wouldn't come. The only thing she could imagine were the red sparks flying from the barrel of a .357 Magnum.

The persistent knock at the door woke Caitlyn, despite her attempts to ignore it. Soon, the person knocking left the door and found the window to her bedroom. She didn't know how long she'd been sleeping, but she knew she couldn't sleep through the persistent knocking. She stumbled to her feet, screaming at the irritating visitor.

"Who is it?" Caitlyn swung the door open and scowled at her sister, whose expression mirrored her own troubled face. Caitlyn left the door open and went to sit down at the kitchen table. Cathleen entered and sat opposite her.

"What's up, sis?" Cathleen asked.

Caitlyn said, "The question is, what are you doing here?"

"I know something is seriously wrong with you, Lyn," she said, calling Caitlyn by her childhood nickname. "I haven't been able to sleep, you know, I guess it's the twin thing."

"I'm fine. Just fine. You could have called. You didn't have to drive 2000 miles to ask me that."

"If I'd called, you would have lied, like you're doing now. So, you might as well tell me, because I'm not leaving until you do. I know something is very wrong and I want to know what it is."

"Did the spirits tell you? Or was it your crystal ball?"

Cathleen took her sister's hand and looked into her eyes, "As a matter of fact, it was the spirits."

Caitlyn felt tears burning in her eyes for the first time since the beginning of her ordeal. Cathleen rose and instinctively started to make tea. She knew where everything was, as if it were her own kitchen. Caitlyn began to tell her sister about Mark and Theresa.

"So what are you going to do?" Cathleen questioned. "He's made his decision."

"I'm not taking this lying down. I've worked and sacrificed too much, thinking that we would be retiring together and living the good life after Jason was finished with school."

"Lyn, the first thing you need to do is to get an attorney. Mark may leave, but you need to know your legal rights."

"Forget an attorney. I'm getting a gun, and I'm going to take back what belongs to me."

"Are you crazy? You must have lost your ever- loving mind! A human being, a man can't belong to any woman, except his mother, maybe. You make him sound like a pair of shoes or an umbrella. I know this is hard, but if he wants to go, you can't stop him."

"To hell with that! I invested too many years with that man … working double shifts to make ends meet, putting up with his crazy family and taking care of him and his son."

"But, Lyn, from the sound of it, Theresa's invested time in him, too. You both have. Don't give him the satisfaction of seeing you two fight in the street like common hoodlums. Besides, if you kill him, what's that going to do to Jason?"

"Jason will be all right, you'll see to that."

"Jason would be wounded, and he might not ever recover from this. He doesn't need to visit his parents in the graveyard or in prison. You've always told him that violence only creates more violence. Are you going to be a hypocrite?"

"I'm not a hypocrite, but I'm not going to let that woman come in and steal my husband."

"She's not stealing your husband. Didn't you say he was packing the car? He didn't have a gun to his head, he wanted to leave . . ."

"He is my husband for better or for worse, until death does us part."

"Lyn, he made a decision. I know it's hard, especially after all those years, but you're going to have to pull it together, just like I did when Stanley died. For months, I just wanted to crawl into my bed, devour one more carton of Ben and Jerry's Chunky Monkey and, then, just die. I made it through the pain and so will you. Tomorrow, we are going to get you a good attorney." Cathleen hugged her sister with a knowing that most humans couldn't describe.

*****

Cathleen sat on the plush leather sofa at Bates, Bates and Bartholomew, Attorneys at Law. Caitlyn had left the hospital in plenty of time to meet her sister, but on the way she stopped by Carter's to pick up her gun. She loved the way the cold steel felt in her hand.

1 .   Caitlyn is
   A.   Going to have to find a way to get even with Mark and Theresa.
   B.   Going to have to take matters into her own hands if she's going to get Mark back.
   C.   Going to have to resign herself to being single and taking care of herself.

2 .   Caitlyn's next step should be
   A.   To hire the meanest divorce lawyer she can find.
   B.   To plot the perfect murder.
   C.   To get a good Therapist.

3 .   Caitlyn should
   A.   Divorce Mark and take everything.
   B.   Try to get Mark to come home and save her twenty-three year long marriage.
   C.   Focus on herself and her son.

4 .   Caitlyn should call Jason and
   A.   Tell him about his father and get him on her side.
   B.   Tell him that they've been deserted by his father
   C.   Sit down with him and Mark to talk openly and honestly with him.

5 .   Caitlyn should

A.   Pack up Mark's things, take them to Theresa's house and make a scene.

B.   Destroy his things or have a garage sale.

C.   Set a time for Mark to pick-up his belongings and then change the locks.

6.   Caitlyn should

A.   Start to date one of Mark's closest friends or a family member.

B.   Cook a great meal, dress up in sexy clothes, invite Mark over and seduce him.

C.   Take some time before she thinks about romance.

7.   Caitlyn should

A.   Hold on to the house and make Mark pay through the nose.

B.   Break things or make up reasons to have Mark come over to the house.

C.   Sell the house and start over.

8.   Caitlyn should

A.   Pretend to be sick and leave her job to make Mark pay more money.

B.   Remind Mark of their plans and let him know how much she needs him.

C.   Sit down with her lawyer, figure out what's fair, and divorce him.

9 .   Caitlyn should
   A.   Write a letter about Theresa to the school board in Bay City.
   B.   Ask Mark to go to marriage counseling with her.
   C.   Leave Mark and Theresa alone.

1 0 .   Caitlyn should
   A.   Tell Mark's family off and never speak to any of them again.
   B.   Ask Mark's mother to talk him into coming home to her.
   C.   Remind herself that these people are still a part of Jason's family.

1 1 .   Caitlyn should
   A.   Make sure that Mark and Theresa don't have a moment's peace.
   B.   Attempt to scare Mark and Theresa with her new gun.
   C.   Try to get on with her life.

If your answers total
   Mostly A's read ending X
   Mostly B's read ending Y
   Mostly C's read ending Z

Ending X

Cathleen stood up suddenly, nearly dropping the coffee cup resting on her lap. The tingling in her arms was hot; the pain almost made her scream. The receptionist looked after her as Cathleen flew out of the law office, with a frantic look on her face. Cathleen didn't know where to go, she would have to let her intuition take her where she needed to be.

Growing up, everyone had laughed at her-- including Caitlyn. They had called her space cadet, but her predictions had always seemed to ring true. And, now, she knew her sister was in serious trouble. Caitlyn hadn't answered her cell phone to provide a clue as to where to find her.

As Cathleen made her way to the freeway entrance ramp, she remembered Caitlyn saying something about a house on Scott Street. As she was about to pull into the Chevron Station for directions, she saw the sign identifying Scott Street as the exit. After a mile or so, she spotted Caitlyn's car parked haphazardly across the front of the driveway of a little yellow house with white trim. The yard was filled with beautiful blooming flowers, and flowerbeds outlined with white rocks. Cathleen jumped out of the car. It lurched forward, almost knocking her down. She had to grab the door to jump back in and put it in park. She ran to the door, where she saw Caitlyn shouting at Mark, with Theresa cowering behind him. Children were screaming and tears were rolling down Caitlyn's face. Cathleen could hear sirens approaching; she slowly moved toward her sister.

"Caitlyn, please give me the gun. You don't want to do this."

Cathleen wanted to distract Caitlyn, so she thought she'd try to use the one person that Caitlyn loved more that she hated Mark.

"I talked to Jason, earlier," Cathleen said, moving closer to her sister. "I thought it would be a good idea for you to take a short trip and visit him for a day or two. What do you think? Can you get the time off?"

"Get out of my way," Caitlyn shouted. "I'm going to kill this bastard and his bitch."

Cathleen searched her mind for something—anything to distract her sister.

"Jason is so funny. He has a girlfriend. He says she looks like us. Isn't that funny?"

Cathleen eased her body between Mark and Caitlyn, waving them backwards with one hand, but they were too scared to move. The volume of the children's screams, the television, the noisy washer, and the approaching sirens were deafening. Cathleen started to pray softly as she walked toward her sister, one step at a time, trying not to make any sudden moves that would scare her. Caitlyn had silent tears pouring out down her checks.

Cathleen moving closer to her sister, and began to recite. "The Lord is my Shepherd, I shall not want. He makes me lie down in green pastures, say it with me, Lyn." It was the scripture they had learned as children, and their mother had told them to say it whenever they were scared.

"He leads me beside still waters. Lyn, you're not praying with me! He restores my soul. . . He leads me in the path of righteousness. Lyn Pray with me please!!"

"Put the gun down!!" The cop screamed. "Officer needs back-up at 2315 Scott Street."

"Lyn, pray, please. For his name's sake. Even though I walk through the Valley of the Shadow of Death. Lyn, give me the gun. I shall fear no evil. Give me the gun."

"Ma'am, move away from her," the officer said.

Cathleen had seen the scene play out in her mind, and she couldn't allow it to happen. With each word, she took a step closer to her sister. The police had guns drawn, sirens were still screeching, but Cathleen continued. She ignored the shouts of the policeman.

"For though art with me."

As the policeman took aim, Cathleen heard the click of his pistol as he cocked it. She lurched forward and took the gun out of her sister's hand. With one hand, she handed the gun to the cop; with the other, she grabbed her sister and hugged her. Caitlyn's sobs shook them both. A red-faced policeman with a potbelly grabbed Caitlyn and threw her to the floor.

"Please, don't hurt her, she's my wife," Mark screamed, still holding onto Theresa.

"You have the right to remain silent, anything you say may be used against you in a court of law . . ." the cop said, as he was handcuffing her.

"Caitlyn, pray with me. Our Father who art in heaven . . . " Cathleen continued.

This time, Cathleen could hear her sister's weary voice. Her long hair covered her face, and her body could not move under its own power. The cops lifted her and moved her limp body toward the waiting police car. The neighbors were outside whispering and speculating.

Cathleen got as close as she could to her sister. "Keep praying, don't stop. Don't say anything other than your prayers."

Caitlyn looked dazed as the policeman guided her, head first, into the police car. Mark watched with tears in his eyes as the police car, with Caitlyn in it, pulled away. As the scene cleared and after the police had all the statements, Cathleen moved Caitlyn's still running car to the curb.

Mark said, "Do you want me to drive her car home?"

"No, Mark. I think you've done enough for everybody."

"Why are you so angry with me? She is the one that came barging in here like Rambo."

"Surely you don't think you're the 'victim.' It was your decision that set this all into motion. You weren't man enough to control your urges. You could have divorced her so you could follow your penis around. You lied for over ten years, and you think you're the victim? Mark, this is just the beginning of your troubles. All actions have consequences and from where I sit, you have ten years worth of lies, deceit and betrayal coming your way. Now, if you will excuse me, I have to see after my sister. Why don't you go see after your wife and children?"

Mark stood and watched, the hair on his neck standing at attention. Not knowing how to respond, he knew first-hand about Cathleen's predictions.

*****

The jury of eight men and four women took less than two hours to convict Caitlyn of aggravated assault for shooting up Marguerite's car and holding Mark and Theresa at gunpoint. Jason and Cathleen sat quietly as the verdict was read. Caitlyn was sentenced to eighteen months in jail, and anger management classes, but Caitlyn's greatest punishment was the sadness in Jason's eyes.

Ending Y

Cathleen was relieved to see her sister walk through the door. She had been praying relentlessly because she knew that her sister was on the brink of disaster. Attorney Bates' secretary ushered the women into his office. He took his glasses off, and looked from one to the other. They were used to people reacting to them that way. The conversation was easy, especially when Attorney Bates asked his brother to step in for a minute. It was funny to have four people in a room, but only two faces. The Brothers Bates were a little younger, but remarkably successful. Caitlyn went against her sister's suggestion to end the marriage quickly and harmoniously. Caitlyn had decided to fight dirty. She wanted Mark and Theresa to feel her wrath. The Bates brothers were willing to go all twelve rounds because, with each round, their paycheck increased. It was a dirty battle, littered with motions and one brief after another.

By the time the lawyers were finished and the divorce was final, Mark and Theresa were both working second jobs to keep up with the legal expenses. Caitlyn didn't fare much better: the money that she got from Mark's retirement had been used up and she had to borrow money from the credit union to keep her house, but it was worth it in her mind. She knew how much Mark was suffering. The bitterness had taken control, and no matter how much Cathleen tried to reason with Caitlyn, she would not listen. Bitterness was making its way into every part of her life. There were complaints from hospital staff. She was always angry; she got into arguments with the neighbors, friends, and even the checkout girl at the grocery store. Jason was the one who was most affected by his mother's constant anger.

"Mom, would you come in here for a minute?" he called from the kitchen.

Caitlyn waddled in, wearing the faded yellow bathrobe with the blue and pink stars that were now white. Before she could speak, she saw her son sitting at the table with his aunt and her best friend, Sharon.

"What the hell is this? Did somebody die?"

Sharon spoke first. "Yes, someone did die. The woman we all knew as Caitlyn."

Caitlyn burst into laughter. She turned to go back to her room as Jason ran to stand between her and the door.

"Get out of my way, Jason, you're not too big for me to put across my knee."

"Yes, I am, Mom. But that is beside the point. Mom, you can't go on like this. We are all hurting, watching you. Dad was wrong for what he did, but you have got to let it go."

His eyes started to water. "I need my mom back. I lost my dad and you're destroying my mom."

Caitlyn walked past him, but she could tell that he was crying when he said, "Please, Mom, don't turn your back on me. Do you hate me like you hate Dad?"

The question stopped Caitlyn in her tracks. She turned to look at her son and really saw him for the first time in almost two years. She walked toward him and grabbed his head, pulling it toward her shoulder as his tears spilled over.

"I'm sorry, sweet boy. I didn't know how much I was hurting you. I apologize, can you forgive me?"

It was almost as if Caitlyn had had cataracts removed from her eyes. She saw clearly all the pain in her son's eyes and the look on her sister's face; that look that she always got when she was scared or nervous.

"Mom, I forgive you . . ."

"Sssh, Jason sometimes parents can act like children, and I'm really sorry."

"It's okay, Mom. Can you come and sit and talk to us? We have something we want to tell you."

Jason, Sharon, and Cathleen each told Caitlyn what she meant to them. There were laughter and tears, and afterwards, a spark of the real Caitlyn was beginning to show through--not the unkempt woman, now forty pounds heavier. Cathleen had made chicken enchiladas, black beans, and wild rice. Sharon had brought her chocolate sweet potato pie, with warm rum sauce. The foursome ate and talked. Sharon put on an old Phil Collins record and Jason brought out the Scrabble game. "Mourn" on a triple word score was enough to yield the game to Caitlyn, and at that moment, for Caitlyn, the mourning was over. She realized she had the love she needed.

Ending Z

Caitlyn stood at the counter in the gun shop. The waiting period for her gun purchase was over. The gun clerk with the southern drawl eyed her suspiciously. He noticed Caitlyn's hands trembled as she rolled the cold steel gun around in her hand.

After a couple of minutes, she felt a shiver that ran up her spine as she thought of the crying mothers, wives, siblings and girlfriends that came to hospitals to see the lifeless corpses of husbands, sons, brothers and boyfriends with bullet holes in them. She didn't want to be the kind of monster that inflicted that kind of pain, even though Mark's family may have deserved it. She put the gun in her pocket and went to meet her sister.

"Hey, I'm sorry I'm late. I had to run an errand," Caitlyn said, as she opened the door and saw her sister seated in the attorney's office.

Cathleen eyed Caitlyn warily as the door opened and a slight woman, well less than five feet tall, came to greet them. She looked liked she was playing dress up in her mother's heels and pearls. The slight lady introduced herself and showed them to a sparsely furnished office dominated by a huge cherry wood desk. There were pictures lying against the wall and fabric swatches that designers use. Boxes in neat rows lined the walls.

"Just moving in?" Cathleen asked

"No, I've been here for five years."

With that, Dorothy Bates sat in her big chair with her feet dangling. She grabbed the sides of the chair to push herself under the desk. With a flint of a smile-mixed frown, she took out a folder marked 'Caitlyn Montgomery vs. Mark Montgomery.' At the sight of it, Caitlyn felt sick in the pit of her stomach. Dorothy Bates was emotionless. She gathered facts and gave Caitlyn a list of items to bring to their next meeting. The meeting was brief and Dorothy Bates was matter of fact. As they were leaving, Dorothy's face softened a fraction of an inch. She said, "Don't worry. I'll take care of this. You'll be just fine."

The two sisters walked hand in hand to the parking lot. Cathleen drove her sister to a little two-story beige office building with a 'For Sale' sign out front. Cathleen turned to her sister.

"Lyn, I made an appointment for you to speak with a grief counselor. Divorce can be just as devastating as a death. It'll do you good to talk to someone about the divorce and how your life is going to change."

Caitlyn was too weak to argue. The sessions went well, and for once Caitlyn started to come to grips with her divorce. She knew she'd have to tell Jason. Summer school would be over in a couple of days and he'd be home.

*****

Jason dropped the large duffle bag stuffed with dirty clothes on the floor as he entered the backdoor. It was a choreographed dance of hollering, "Mom," opening the refrigerator and picking up the phone. He stopped mid-holler when he saw his aunt sitting at the kitchen table. He was the only person who never had trouble telling them apart.

"Aunt Leen, what are you doing here? Where's mom?"

"Well, hello to you, too, college boy."

"College man," Jason replied, stroking the erupting beard forming around his chin.

"Sorry, college man. I stand corrected." They laughed as Cathleen got up to give her nearly 6-foot nephew a hug.

"Your mom is on her way home. She went to get a few of your favorites from the store. We didn't expect you until this evening."

"I finished my exam early and headed home for something good to eat. Can you make me those chocolate caramel brownies that I love?"

"Look in the microwave."

"All right," Jason said with a smile, taking the plate of brownies and going to the fridge to get the milk, drinking directly from the carton.

"Where's Dad?"

Cathleen sat silently. "That sounds like your mom now."

Caitlyn practically skipped up the driveway when she saw Jason's beat up Honda Civic sitting in the driveway. It had been almost five months since she'd seen her son.

She burst in the door, "Where's my boy?"

She hugged him tightly, and he didn't try to move away. College had made him appreciate his mom's hugs.

"Where's Dad?"

Caitlyn's expression changed.   As she took a seat at the table, Cathleen looked away. Caitlyn gave her son a weak smile, and tried not to meet his eyes.

"Well, baby your Dad doesn't live here anymore. We are getting a divorce . . ."

"That's good, Mom.   Dad doesn't deserve someone as wonderful as you."

Caitlyn and Cathleen shared a quick, questioning glance.

"What do you mean?" Caitlyn couldn't hide the shock on her face

"Dad is selfish. I knew you would find out about Theresa and Morgan sooner or later."

"How did you know, Jason?"

"I overheard Grandma talking to Aunt Robyn and I've heard dad talking to Theresa when you were at work. Then, there was this one time I saw Morgan and Theresa when Dad took me to the mall. Morgan ran up to him screaming, 'Daddy, Daddy.' He tried to tell me that he must look like her daddy. He picked her up, and I could tell they looked a lot alike, and Theresa looked really nervous. It made me wonder about it, so I followed him one night, while you were at work. And I saw him use the garage door opener to go in her house."

"How long have you known?"

"About four years or so."

"Why didn't you tell me?"

"I didn't want to make you unhappy. I know how much you love Dad and me."

Caitlyn kissed her son's worried look away.

"Thanks, Jay. You did the right thing," she said.

She got up and started to make the Chicken Spaghetti that her son loved so much, she looked at him. To her he still was four years old.

"How did I get so lucky to get a son like you?" she said

"I don't know, maybe it was a miracle. I guess God smiled on you."

They both laughed and caught up on all the news as they played Scrabble with Cathleen.

*****

The day the divorce was final was a day that Caitlyn would never forget. She discovered that Mark had resources that she had never known about. Thanks to a bulldog of a lawyer with exceptional computer skills, Mark's assets were found and Caitlyn was left quite comfortable, due to the divorce settlement. But, that wasn't why she would remember the day. She was sitting in the hospital cafeteria when Dr. Malone came and sat across from her.

"Well, today was the day wasn't it?"

"Yes, as of 10:00 am, I became a free agent."

"How do you feel?" Dr. Malone asked.

"Relieved, mostly, but a little apprehensive. I haven't been single since I was nineteen and even then I wasn't single because I had dated Mark since I was fifteen."

"Well, I hope you won't have to date too much." Dr. Malone looked her in the eyes for a long moment, and then continued. "I've been jealous of your husband for fifteen years and I don't want to be jealous of your dates, too. I know we've been friends and you might not see me as anything other than a friend, but, will you please consider me when you start to think about dating?"

Caitlyn looked shocked. Dr. Malone said, "Surely you had to know, I thought I tried not to be too obvious, but everyone else seems to have noticed."

"Well, Adam, a lot of things have gone over my head lately. But, what about Friday night?"

"Friday night?"

"Yes, I'd like you to come to dinner at my place Friday night."

Adam's smile lit up the room, "Can I bring the wine? What time? Can I help you cook?"

"Yes, wine will be fine, 7:00 p.m. And if you'd like to help me cook be there at 6:00. Do you play Scrabble?"

"Yes, I love Scrabble."

Caitlyn was excited. When she allowed herself time to consider his revelation, she realized that she had feelings for Adam. They had worked together for years, he was her friend, and they laughed easily and often. Over the last year she had cried on his shoulders many times. He beat her at Scrabble, which was a feat that had to be corrected. They talked and found common ground that became the foundation for the great relationship that they both grew to cherish. The relationship grew steadily and tenderly.

Jason gave Caitlyn away at the candlelight ceremony in the hospital chapel. Adam was the husband that Cathleen had predicted Caitlyn would meet one day. She had not thought about that until she was packing to move to her new house. In a box of old childhood artwork she found a picture her sister had given her when they were fourteen. The picture was of a white Tudor style house, with a circular driveway, beautiful gardens and sculptured hedges. A couple was standing in the entry way and the caption underneath said, "Adam, the doctor, will take you to places that you have never dreamed of and make you happier than you ever thought humanly possible. He'll be a soul mate and friend." At that moment, Caitlyn realized her sister was truly gifted and she was very grateful.

Dedra

Dedra smoothed her chiffon print dress over her nearly-ready-to-deliver, pregnant stomach as she heard her name being called by the prosecutor to take the witness stand. Her hair was done up in wispy curls that fell across her pretty oval-shaped face. Her make-up accented the pregnant glow. Dedra was twenty-eight, but she looked barely old enough to drive. She approached the witness stand slowly and deliberately, looking earnestly in the direction of the jury. She listened intently as she was sworn in and agreed to tell the truth, the whole truth and nothing but the truth. The prosecutor was a red-faced little man who reminded her of Barney from the Andy Griffith show.

"Would you state your full name for the court?"

"My name is Dedra Renee Donaldson."

"And where do you reside?"

"I live at 5245 Apple Valley Court, Atlanta, Georgia."

"And Ms. Donaldson, how long have you lived at this address?"

"I've lived there for three and half years."

"And who resides at that residence with you?"

"My daughter Asya and my fiancé Keith Myers."

"And Miss Donaldson, where were you on the evening of October 8th, 1998 between 8:00 pm and 11:00 pm?"

"Keith and I were riding around the city looking at houses referred to us by our real estate agent. We are looking for a bigger house, since we are expecting a second child."

Dedra patted her stomach as she glanced at Keith, and then back to the prosecutor.

"How can you be so sure of the time, Ms. Donaldson?"

"I'm sure because we watched The Practice before we left home to go look at the houses."

"Ms. Donaldson, don't you think it was odd to look at houses in the dark?"

"No sir. Keith and I both worked until 5:00 pm. The realtor told us to narrow down the list of houses to three or four, and she would show us the ones we chose on Saturday morning."

"And you are absolutely sure you were with Keith on the evening of October 8th, between the hours of eight and eleven?"

"Yes sir, I am one hundred percent sure."

"Ms. Donaldson, do you know what the term 'perjury' means?"

"Yes, sir. I do."

"Do you also know that you can be sentenced to prison for making perjuries statements while under oath?"

"Yes Sir."

"Ms. Donaldson, I'll ask you again, where were you on the night of October 8, 1998?"

"Objection, that question has already been asked and answered by the witness."

"Overruled."

"Ms. Donaldson, where were you on October 8, 1998?"

"I was riding around looking for houses with Keith, as I stated previously."

"Ms. Donaldson, isn't it true that you were at home with your daughter, waiting on Keith to return so that you could go looking at houses?"

"No sir, that is not true. We were looking for houses."

"Ms. Donaldson, was anyone else residing at your house that night?"

"No, sir."

"Well, can you explain the eleven phone calls made from your home phone between eight and eleven o'clock that evening?"

"Well, my sister has a key. She may have come in while we were gone."

"Ms. Donaldson, can you explain why your sister would have called three of Keith's friends and his mother?"

"Ah . . . she might have been trying to find us?"

"Do you have a cell phone, Ms. Donaldson?"

"Yes, sir."

"Does your sister have your cell phone number?"

"I'm not sure."

"Ms. Donaldson, again, I ask you, do you know the penalty for perjury?"

"Objection. Counselor is badgering the witness."

"Overruled."

Dedra rubbed her stomach and tried to calm her heartbeat. She was sure it could be heard by anyone in a hundred mile radius.

"Yes sir, I do."

"Ms. Donaldson, are you familiar with a restaurant called Pizza Palace?"

"Yes sir, I am."

"Ms. Donaldson, can you explain the charge made to your credit card to the Pizza Palace on the night in question and the entry in the delivery log at 8:55 pm on the night in question?"

"Yes sir, I guess we left later than 8 o'clock because we ate Pizza in the car as we were riding around."

"Ms. Donaldson, can you explain the statements made by Mrs. Murray who lives across the street? She said that she brought you some mail that had been left in her box by mistake at around 9 pm that evening. A statement from three of Keith's co-workers indicate that you called them looking for him because he hadn't arrived home and was not answering his cell phone?"

"Sir, they must have been mistaken."

"Ms. Donaldson, are you saying . . . "

"Objection. Counselor is leading the witness!"

"Overruled."

"Ms. Donaldson, is it your testimony that the phone company, the credit card company, Pizza Palace, the delivery man, Mrs. Murray and three of Keith's friend are all mistaken?"

Dedra fought back the tears that were determined to carve their way down her flawlessly made-up face. The baby was kicking like crazy—as if it sensed imminent danger.

"Yes sir, I believe they are mistaken. I thought we left directly after The Practice was over, but maybe it was later, because we did get the pizza and the mail before we left."

"Ms. Donaldson, does Keith have a car?"

"Yes, he does."

"What kind of car is it, Ms. Donaldson?"

"It's a 1996 Pontiac Firebird."

"What color is it?"

"Red."

"And where does he usually park the car?"

"He parks in the yard."

"Was it there on the night of October 8th?"

"Yes, it was."

"Ms. Donaldson, are you sure? Mrs. Murray has testified that it was not there when she brought the mail, and Mr. Farmer, the gentleman who delivered your pizza, agrees with her."

"Objection. Calling for a conclusion from the witness. She can't testify to what they saw or didn't see"

"Sustained."

"Ms. Donaldson, can you explain why three of the eleven calls made from your residence were to your fiancée's cell phone—if you were with him."

"I'm not sure, like I said. It may have been my sister looking for us."

"Ms. Donaldson, can you also explain why Keith's cell phone call to your residence at 10:15 on the night in question, was picked up by a cell phone tower twenty-seven miles from your residence and four blocks from the scene of the crime?"

"Objection."

"Overruled."

"No sir, I cannot explain it. Keith must have lost his cell phone. He is always losing it."

"Ms. Donaldson, it is also the testimony from Ms. Murray and Mr. Snow, your next door neighbor to the left, that Keith did not return to your residence until 10:45 pm. They remember because of the loud music on his car radio when he returned, and the argument that ensued as he entered the premises at 5245 Apple Valley court."

"Ms. Donaldson, the court did not hear your answer."

At that moment, Dedra lost her resolve. The dam of tears broke free and found their way out, leaving tracks and crevices on her flawless face.

"Your Honor, if it pleases the court, may we take a short recess so the witness can regain her composure?" asked Keith's lawyer

"It's 11:20. Let's reconvene after lunch at 1:00 pm," the judge decided.

*****

Dedra's jail cell was filled with pictures cut from magazines, sales circulars, and newspapers. She was getting through prison days by decorating her future house and choosing a wardrobe that would never again include the color orange. Her cell was filled with pictures, of furniture for the dining room, wallpaper, and candlesticks. Each child's room, bathroom and even the outdoor patio had been furnished in Dedra's mind and on her wall. On holidays and birthdays, she had picked out dresses, socks, ribbons and bows for herself and the girls and stored them in a shoebox. And, when she imagined conversations with them, they always had on one of the outfits she'd picked out for them. She had always had a great imagination, and could create wonderful fantasy worlds, but had difficulty keeping fantasy out of reality.

"Ded, Chaplin Denton wants to see you," one of the prison guards told her.

"Okay, thanks, Officer Okafor. Do you know what she wants?"

"No, but the warden's secretary was with her."

Dedra's eyes widened. She wondered what was wrong. She put down the magazine and picked up the torn pictures from the floor of her cell. She decided to change into a clean white prison issued tee shirt, combed her hair, and pulled it back into a tight ponytail. She thought of all the reasons why the Chaplain could want to see her; she told herself that nothing else bad could happen. During her three years in prison, her mother had died and her baby had become a ward of the state. Keith had never come to see her and had refused to take custody of their children. Dedra walked slowly to the Chaplain's office, trying to prepare her head for the unknown. Each scenario she imagined was worse than the next. By the time she arrived at the Chaplain's office, she was almost in tears.

"Chaplain Denton, you wanted to see me?"

"Yes, Dedra have a seat."

Chaplain Denton didn't look at her, but continued to shuffle the papers on her desk as she intermittently sipped herbal tea. When the papers were all in the piles she wanted, she looked at Dedra, whose heart was pounding. Dedra thought the news had to be bad, because it seemed that the Chaplain was stalling. To keep her mind busy, Dedra tried to take mental photographs of the Chaplains office.

It looked as if someone had placed office furniture in a green house. Everywhere Dedra looked, there were vines growing. There were probably ten different species of ivy. There were huge pots of cactus and plants, some with blooms, some without. They were by the door, next to the chair, on top of the file cabinets, hanging overhead. Dedra wondered why there were no personal items: photos, degrees, vacation mementoes. The only thing that looked like it belonged to Chaplain Denton was the coffee cup. Chaplain Denton was a sullen-face little woman who never smiled. She had once believed that she could change the world, but her work at the prison stole her hope and replaced it with cynicism. She despised weak women, they reminded her of her mother.

Dedra wondered about her ethnicity; she could have been Italian, Latin, Jewish, or Bi-racial. Her skin looked tanned year-round, and she had long black hair and blacker eyes, which cut to the core.

Chaplain Denton cleared her throat slightly, demanding Dedra's attention.

"Dedra, I've sent for you because the warden has asked me to recommend twelve non-violent inmates to participate in a new rehabilitation program. Completion of the program would mean early release for the prisoners involved. It is a six-month program paid for with federal, state, and private funds. There are four components to the program, and one is counseling. That is where I come in. The second is job skills training and research. The third is a life skills portion, wherein each inmate will learn skills to help her survive on the outside and develop personal standards. The fourth portion of the program is goal-setting and forecasting. Here are the rules and regulations of the program. If you're interested, take some time and review them. Registration will be Thursday between two and four."

"Chaplain, I know I'm interested! I want to sign up now."

"Dedra, that is one of the first lessons in the life skills portion—not to react on impulse. Take your time and review the information. Read it carefully and register on Thursday, after you have reviewed the requirements and expectations."

Dedra went straight to her cell. Missing dinner and recreation time, she read all the papers the chaplain had given her. She kept reading them. Dedra couldn't believe that she could be getting out soon. In six months, she could be holding her kids in her arms. She paced her cell until her cellmate got angry and threatened to tear every hair from her head if she didn't sit down. Even after lights-out, she tried to focus her eyes and read the papers one more time.

The next day, Dedra dressed quickly, and then asked permission to see the Chaplain instead of going to chow. She waited outside the Chaplain's office for her arrival.

When Chaplain Denton arrived, she looked very irritated to see Dedra.

She said over her shoulder as she walked by her, "The second life skills lesson is to follow instructions. The instructions said that if you wanted to register for the program, you were to sign the enrollment form and take it to the warden's secretary between two and four pm on Thursday—not, 'bring it to my office on Tuesday.' Now, excuse me, Dedra. I have work to do."

Dedra could barely contain herself; every few minutes, she touched the papers to make sure they had not fallen from her pocket. She got in trouble at work because she was not taking care of the dishes that came to her from the conveyor belt. Twice, plates had tumbled to the floor; and Big Lovely had gotten in her face. Big Lovely was 6'3" 330 lbs, and far from lovely by any stretch of the imagination. She was doing life for torturing and murdering the man who had killed her father. When Big Lovely found out the drunk driver had been convicted of driving under the influence three times before he killed her father, she decided he would not live to kill again. At the prison, Big Lovely was Head Kitchen Trustee and she ran the kitchen with an iron fist. Dedra avoided Big Lovely because she knew she could be trouble.

Dedra barely managed to get through the day. Thursday, at fifteen minutes before 2:00 pm, Dedra asked the guard for permission to go to the Warden's office. She arrived just as Beverly, the Warden's secretary, was packing up her lunch. Dedra waited until she was acknowledged and told her why she was there.

Beverly smiled at her and said, "Good for you."

Dedra genuinely liked Beverly. Beverly had been really nice to her when her mother died, even giving her permission to skip work detail the day of the funeral. Rumor had it that Beverly had been an inmate, herself, but it was hard to imagine that this graceful bejeweled woman had ever adorned a prison uniform. Beverly gave Dedra another stack of papers to read and sign. Dedra sat in the cushiony leather chair and breathed in a fragrance that reminded her of Christmas—or maybe the thought of getting out of prison felt like Christmas. Beverly's office was warm with a large landscape picture behind her head in a big silver frame. Her desk was dark mahogany wood, with matching credenza and file cabinets. It could have been any bank president's office. Pictures of cats, different cats, were alternating on her computer screensaver.

Dedra had longed for the day when she would be in Keith's arms again, the two of them watching their children play. She wondered what Chyna looked like; she had been three months old when Dedra had to give her up. Dedra didn't know what she'd go home to, but she thought she'd trade the outside nightmare for the nightmare of prison life anytime. After the horrors she'd seen in prison, she would do anything to get out: even if it meant giving up an arm or a leg.

Dedra showed up ten minutes early for her first counseling session with Chaplain Denton. She was very matter-of-fact and showed no compassion, which Dedra found odd for a Chaplain.

After Chaplain Denton got the papers on her desk in exactly the right order, she pulled out a file and looked intently at Dedra.

"Why are you here, Ms. Donaldson?"

Dedra stammered, "I got a note that my counseling sessions would be at 3:00 pm, today."

"Counseling session—not sessions." She continued in an irritated tone, "I know what time your SESSION was scheduled, Ms. Donaldson, my question refers to your daily address in the Georgia State Prison System. In other words, MS. DONALDSON, why are you here in prison?"

Dedra hadn't expected that question. She'd expected to relay how sorry she was for what she'd done, how it would never happen again, and how she planned to be a model citizen from that point on. Dedra could barely swallow the lump in her throat. Chaplain Denton's eyes stared at her; they seemed to be growing stormier by the second. Dedra wouldn't have been surprised if she'd reached out and slapped her, by the look on the Chaplain's face.

"They convicted me of perjury during my fiancée's trial, and I was sentenced to ten years—"

"Did they," Chaplain Denton interrupted. "Or did you, by your actions, convict yourself? And to whom do you refer to as THEY?"

Dedra thought, This is not going to be as easy as I thought.

"I guess you could say I convicted myself."

"What is more important is what would you say, Ms. Donaldson."

"The District Attorney filed perjury charges against me. As a result of my false statements in court during the trial of Keith Myers, my fiancé, I was sentenced to ten years."

"Fiancé?   And what was the scheduled date of the marriage?"

Dedra lowered her eyes. "We hadn't set a date, but we'd been together for eight years and he said he was going to marry me."

"Did you have an engagement ring?"

"No, Ma'am. We were saving for it."

Chaplain Denton broke into dry laughter that didn't affect her cold eyes.

"You didn't have a ring? He'd been sharing your bed for eight years, fertilizing your eggs, growing children in your womb, and he never could get around to buying a ring or setting a date? Is that correct?"

Dedra sat silent, feeling the sting of the Chaplin's words.

Chaplin Denton feverishly tapped numbers into her calculator, then sat back in her chair, took a long deep breath and let out a satisfied sigh—as if she had accomplished something great, like finding a cure for cancer. She took the tape from the calculator and looked at it for several seconds before handing it to Dedra.

"You mean to tell me that in 2920 days he couldn't save fifty cents a day to even buy you a ring? He couldn't save the price of a coke, or even a dime a day? If he couldn't buy a ring in all that time, why couldn't he find time to circle a date on a calendar and take you to the local Justice of the Peace?"

Chaplain Denton let out an amused chuckle. Dedra felt the sting of approaching tears, but prison had taught her to control them.

"He wanted it to be perfect."

This time the Chaplain broke out into genuine laughter. As Dedra tried to control her tears, she could feel her chances of getting out of prison fading. She tried to concentrate on a spot on the wall above the Chaplain's head. After a hearty laugh, the Chaplain asked.

"And what happened to your fiancé after you decided to give him ten more years of your life?"

"His case was dismissed because the girl he was on trial for raping refused to testify. She had a nervous breakdown and, since she was a minor, her parents didn't want to put her through a trial. She had to be placed in a mental institution."

Chaplin Denton's eyes shot daggers in Dedra's direction. "You lied to protect a pedophile?"

Dedra's anger was beginning to surface. She snapped, as she spoke. "I know Keith was innocent! He wouldn't do that."

The Chaplain's eyes hardened, as if storm clouds were about to empty themselves all over Dedra. She spoke in a very controlled tone.

"Tell me, Ms. Donaldson, where was he on that fateful night, and what proof do you have that he did not commit this crime?"

The Chaplain noticed Dedra's balled fist, and that made her smile even more.

"I don't know where he was. He said he was just riding around. He had had a bad day and he wanted to cool down before he came home. He told me that the police would never believe him because of the problems he had had when he was a juvenile, so he told me to say that he had been with me."

"The problems of being charged with rape of his twelve year-old neighbor when he was sixteen?"

"Yes. Keith was dating her and she was afraid to tell her father, so she let him be arrested for rape."

"Always someone else's fault, you and Keith the ultimate victims!"

Dedra sat silent, her own storm clouds brewing.

"How to you explain his DNA on the victim and the victim's blood on his underwear?"

"The crime lab has made so many errors. You can't believe those tests. I think they were trying to railroad him for a crime he didn't commit."

"Oh, the crime lab wanted him behind bars, I see. But, why was his car seen near her house and a call from his cell phone placed him four blocks from the victim's residence?"

When Dedra didn't answer, Chaplain Denton fired another question at her.

"Was he ever violent with you?"

"Not really…"

"Not Really? What does that mean?"

"He slapped me a couple of times, but he didn't mean to. He was drinking and upset."

Chaplain Denton looked at Dedra and then pulled out several papers from her file.

"Didn't he, in fact, go to jail for beating you, breaking two ribs and giving you a concussion? And on another occasion, didn't he drag you up the street by your hair, leaving all the skin scrapped from your right arm and thigh? And how many other incidents of violence have there been wherein the police were not called?"

Dedra didn't answer for fear that she'd jump across the desk and beat the hell out of the little witch who sat opposite her. Chaplain Denton continued to taunt her.

"How many times has he visited you while you've been here for lying to protect his ass?"

"He said he can't see me like this."

Chaplain Denton started to laugh, again. This time the laughter was genuine and her eyes watered as she pounded her fist on her knee. She had given up traditional counseling methods long ago after everything she had heard over the years. She wanted Dedra to feel stupid, she wanted Dedra to get off fantasy island. This time, the laughter reminded Dedra of all the times that she'd felt stupid growing up with a near-perfect sister. Whenever she'd tried to join conversations between her sister and her friends, they'd made fun of her comments.

After several seconds, the Chaplain abruptly stopped laughing.

"Get the hell out of my office. You're not ready to tell the truth to yourself, so you definitely can't tell it to me. Get out of my sight and don't come back in here again." The Chaplain groaned through clenched teeth, venom dripping from her eyes, "You're too stupid to live. THEY should have given you life, as far as I'm concerned."

Dedra sat stunned at the Chaplain's words; she didn't know what to do. She would have attacked her, had she been able to get her hands or feet to move. Chaplain Denton rose to her feet and shouted at her. "I said, get the hell out of my office, now!"

Dedra stumbled to her feet as the guard opened the door to see what was going on.

"Get her out of here. It makes me sick to look at her."

The guard grabbed Dedra's arm, unable to believe what had just happened. Dedra seemed to be walking on air as the guard pulled her out of the Chaplain's office. Dedra struggled to get her footing as the guard pushed her forward; causing one of her prison issued white tennis shoes to come off. Even though it was recreation time, the guard took Dedra back to her cell, where she broke down and sobbed—even though she knew it was almost a death sentence to show that kind of weakness in prison. She was hurt and angry; her hopes of early release had been dashed, and she didn't understand why.

Dedra heard the bell that signaled the end of the recreation period. She knew it was time for her to report to work detail, so she tried to pull herself together, to go and face Big Lovely. As she walked in, Big Lovely started to scold her, but took one look at her face and decided against it. Dedra had the look of a woman not to be reckoned with, not even by Big Lovely.

"Girl, what happened to you?" asked Big Lovely.

"I don't want to talk about it!"

"Is it one of your kids? Are they all right?"

Dedra shot her a look that told her to leave it alone. Dedra worked at an intense pace. Everybody around steered clear of her.

When the shift ended, Big Lovely grabbed Dedra's arm and said with more compassion than Dedra could imagine, "Deds, keep your head up. It's going to be okay. It's only time, and time passes."

Big Lovely handed her a small dinner roll that had come from the Warden's dinner. Dedra took it and attempted to smile as she fought back the tears that would have their way. Big Lovely squared her shoulders and stiffened her face.

"Be strong. Do the time, and don't let the time do you."

The next morning, after her breakfast shift, Dedra lied to the guard and said she had to see the Warden's secretary to return some papers for the program she was in. The guard let her through, and she told the same lie at the next three guard stations. She was afraid that when the guard announced her, Beverly would tell that she was lying, and she would be in solitaire for the next ten days. But, Beverly invited her in. Dedra was not sure where to start.

"Do you have a minute?"

"I have about four, as a matter of fact."

Dedra recounted her experience with the Chaplain and asked whether she could have another opportunity to complete the program. Beverly interlaced her fingers, revealing her perfect French manicure and her diamond tennis bracelet.

With a soft Georgia twang that had almost disappeared from her voice, Beverly said, "This program is for women who have learned from their incarceration. It is for women who have chosen to take responsibility for their actions and who have decided not to continue to live on Fantasy Island. The Chaplain and I fought hard for this program. We wrote grants on our personal time to get it here and we are not going to jeopardize it with women who truly do not want to give their all to it."

"I want to give my all…I thought I was."

"Dedra, 'De-Nile' is more than a river in Egypt."

Dedra looked puzzled and Beverly realized that her statement had gone over Dedra's head.

"Dedra, the Chaplain and I believe you are in denial as to why you really landed in prison. You see, it is clear to everyone, other than you, that your decision-making capacity lacks maturity."

"I truly don't understand. Can you give me an example?"

"What is your daughter's name?"

"The oldest is Asya and the youngest is Chyna."

"What would you say if you discovered that Asya was dating a guy who was abusing her, staying out all night and asking her to jeopardize her life for him?"

"I'd make her stop seeing him and tell her that he was no good for her—that she was going to end up dead or in serious trouble if she didn't get rid of him."

"What if she said, 'He really loves me, people just don't understand him'?"

"I'd try to talk to her and make her see that she has to think about her future and do what was best for her."

"Dedra, what was best for you?"

The question took her by surprise.

As the phone rang and interrupted her thoughts, Beverly stood to signal that her time was up. "I'll talk to Chaplain Denton and see if she will give you another chance, and by the way, if you show up here again without a legitimate reason, I will have you thrown into solitaire."

Dedra nodded her head.

Dedra was a zombie for the next several weeks. She began to spend all her free time in the Library or the Chapel. She wrote letter after letter to Keith, even trading meals, soap and toilet paper for postage stamps. She begged him to come and see her; she said she needed to talk to him even though she knew he didn't want to see her there. Her letters got no response until, finally, Keith's mother sent her a letter with a newspaper clipping that was the announcement of Keith's marriage to a woman Dedra didn't know.

She couldn't believe it. There Keith stood, looking dashing in a gray tuxedo with tails, next to this not-so-pleasingly-plumb, woman wearing a strapless gown, showing off her huge breasts and all thirty-two teeth. Dedra thought about how much

Keith had loved it when her breasts got bigger when she was pregnant, and she remembered his disappointment when they went back to their regular size.

Dedra really believed that she was going to die; it was all she could do to get out of bed in the morning. She was so pitiful that the other prisoners didn't even bother to take advantage of her weakness: attacking her was no fun because she didn't even try to fight back. She began to contemplate suicide, but decided that she needed to live long enough to see her girls one more time.

When Big Lovely told Dedra that she would need her help to prepare a graduation luncheon for seven other women who were in the program and being released, she fell prostrate before the altar in the prison chapel and wept until the guards had to remove her. Big Lovely tried to talk to her, she knew what it was like to give up hope and, as quiet as it was kept, she liked Dedra. Unfortunately, no one could reach her. Dedra had lost twenty pounds and now only weighed 115 pounds. She was sent to the infirmary because she had begun to pass out. When it seemed that all hope was lost, a letter came in the mail from Asya saying that her aunt had agreed to bring her to the prison for her eleventh birthday. Dedra didn't want her daughter to see her in such a pathetic state, so she began to eat again, and tried to do something about her appearance. Asya and Chyna were all she had to live for, and it had been more than four years since Dedra had seen her oldest little girl. Dedra had hoped to be home through the early release program, and even though that had not worked out, she was thrilled at the thought of seeing her daughter.

Dedra paced the floor while waiting for the guard to announce that her visitors had arrived. She had not had visitors since her mother died, and that was over two years ago. When the guard brought Dedra into the visitation room, she looked around the room for a little fat cheeked girl with three long brown ponytails. As she looked around the room, her eyes finally found a pair of familiar eyes looking at her; Dedra's sister, Greta, sat with a young lady who looked like a teenager, wearing a miniskirt and boots. She was heading toward her sister when the teenager ran toward her and grabbed her around the waist.

The girl was crying and saying, "Mommy, mommy."

Dedra stopped and pulled herself free and looked into the child's face.

"Asya, is that you, honey?"

"Mommy, don't you recognize me?"

Dedra pulled the child close and didn't say a word. She just held on, kissing the child's head and face.

"I can't believe you're this big! Is that a bra I feel?"

"Of course, Mom! I'm eleven and I wear a 32-A."

Dedra smiled and hung on to her bra-wearing baby. Asya told Dedra about all the things going on in her life. She talked for the whole four-hour visit. It was nearing 6:00, and Dedra knew the visit was going to be over shortly, so she asked her daughter, "When was the last time you saw your father?"

Asya paused. "I don't know, Mom. Probably, three years ago. Auntie and I were in the mall and we saw him. He gave me twenty dollars, but I haven't seen him since."

Asya returned to her stories, as if she had a lifetime of information to tell to her mom before visitation hours were over. In Dedra's fantasy, Keith picked Asya up every weekend and they spent time together. Asya's words about her father forced Dedra out of Fantasy Land. With about ten minutes left in the visit, Dedra asked Asya to excuse her for one minute so that she could speak with Auntie Greta, who was sitting in the corner observing the reunion. Dedra walked over to her sister. She held out her arms and her sister walked into them. They both began to talk at the same time. They had not spoken since the trial; Dedra had been upset when her sister refused to take custody of Chyna. Greta had often warned her sister about Keith.

"Thank you for bringing Asya and for taking care of her. I know how hard it must be. I appreciate it and I'll make it up to you one day, I promise."

"Dedra she's a great kid. On the honor roll, playing soccer and she's learning French."

"She is a great kid, thanks to you. And I understand why you couldn't take Chyna. Having a newborn and trying to finish your degree would have been too much. I'll be grateful to you forever."

"I'm so sorry about all of this," Greta said.

"Don't worry, lil sis, I'm okay," Dedra replied

The two sisters joined hands and walked over to Asya, who was waiting for them. They started to say their goodbyes and promised to write more. Asya clung to her mother as her aunt tried to pry her away. The buzzer sounded and all the prisoners were whisked away. Asya and Greta walked in silence to the car, and Dedra went to her cell and began to write a letter to the Chaplain to beg for a slot in the next early release training program.

Dedra wondered whether it was a coincidence that on her mother's birthday, she received a note from Beverly informing Dedra that she was going to be in the next session of the early release program—after eighteen months of waiting and writing letters. Dedra was ready this time. She finally understood Beverly's statement that 'De-Nile' was more than a river in Egypt."

Dedra arrived at Chaplain Denton's office right on time. She was going to do everything possible to make it, this time. Chaplain Denton had not wanted to admit her again.

She'd told Beverly, "There are too many stupid ass women on the streets all ready. Why should we add Dedra to their numbers?"

Chaplain Denton thought Dedra would probably be eligible for parole in a year or two, anyway. But, Beverly had fought to have her included in this class; there was something about Dedra that reminded Beverly of herself at that age. Chaplain Denton's eyes did not show any emotion as Dedra opened the door to her office. Dedra entered and stood by one of the worn chairs in the Chaplain's office until she was instructed to sit down. After a few seconds of looking Dedra up and down, the Chaplain finally spoke.

"Ms. Donaldson, why are you soaking up the air in my office again?"

Dedra had thought about this question long and hard. She took a breath. "Chaplain, I am here because everyone deserves a second chance. Our last conversation made me think a lot about my life and the mistakes and bad judgments I've made. I'd like to confess my errors and, hopefully, find forgiveness from God, the State of Georgia, and you."

Chaplain Denton was not moved by Dedra's words. After all, everyone finds the Lord in prison. She would find a way to rid herself of the nuisance of this foolish little girl parading around in a woman's body. Dedra continued, after there was no response from the chaplain.

"Since our last conversation, I have come to the conclusion that I am in prison because I chose to love a man more than I loved myself. I chose to put my life, and the lives of my children, at risk because I loved someone who, from his actions, never loved me. I am also here because I refused to listen to the people who had my best interest at heart. I chose to stay in denial and believe that one day he would love me the way I loved him."

The Chaplain could barely hide the shock on her face. Dedra stopped and waited for the next question.

The Chaplain sarcastically replied, "Ms. Donaldson, that is very insightful. What brought you to these conclusions?"

"Chaplain, after our previous conversation, I began to look at my life, not through my eyes, but through the eyes of my daughter, my sister, my mother, my friends—even through your eyes. I tried to be objective, and I realized that it did not make sense for me to be here."

"Then why are you here, Ms. Donaldson?"

"I now realize that I gave all of my personal power to a man who beat me, degraded me, cheated on me and even gave me venereal diseases on more than one occasion. I considered the fact that I have been in this prison for 1736 days—that equals 13,888 hours—and he has never taken the time to visit me. I have received two letters from him. He has not made any attempt to see our children, nor has he sent a dollar to me since I have been here. His actions say that he doesn't love me, regardless of what his lips say. I thought I would die if he ever left me, so I endured the beatings and his involvement with other women."

Dedra hesitated, feeling as if she were seeing a motion picture unfold before her eyes. After a minute or so she continued.

"Now, I can admit to myself and to you, that he was probably guilty of raping both of the girls. I'd never let my mind consider that possibility before now. I thought I could not survive without Keith but now I see that I have survived 1736 days, 13,888 hours and 833,260 minutes and my heart is still beating. Blood is still running through my veins! What I cannot endure is the fact that I have made my children orphans."

Chaplain Denton could not hide her shock this time. It took her a minute to compose her question. Dedra sat with her hands on her lap waiting for the next question.

Finally, Chaplain Denton asked, "And how do you feel about Mr. Myers now?"

Dedra took a deep breath and replied, "I don't hate him, now. My feelings are kind of nondescript. It's not love, it's not hate. He is simply another human being that is breathing the good Lord's air. I have to consider that part of him is in my two girls, and to hate him is to hate a part of them, so frankly Chaplain, I'm still grappling with that one."

Dedra stopped for a few minutes, then continued as the Chaplain looked at her, nodding her approval. "A few months ago, I thought I was going to die. I wrote Keith sixty-seven letters and he never replied to one of them. I guess his mother was tired of me writing, so she sent me his wedding announcement from the local newspaper. He was marrying a dentist and was going to honeymoon in the Bahamas. I thought, 'How could he do this to me?' Then I realized that he wasn't doing anything to me, I was doing it to myself."

The Chaplain, let out a loud, "Amen," but wondered if her response was premature, when she heard Dedra say, "But even with that I still loved him. I still wanted him until I got a letter from my daughter saying that my sister had agreed to bring her to see me for her eleventh birthday. I could hardly believe how big she had gotten. I could see him in her and I still loved him. But, at the end of visiting hours, when I asked my beautiful little girl when she had last seen her father, she couldn't remember. My sister said he has never visited her."

Dedra continued through tears.

"The one time that she saw him was when he was in the mall with another woman. I accepted him neglecting me, but I could not accept him neglecting our child. At that time, something strange happened. It's hard to describe. The only way I can explain it is to compare it to one of those old-fashioned Jack-in-the-Box Toys. Have you ever seen one?"

Chaplain Denton looked a little puzzled, but she answered the question.

"Yes, I think I know the toy you're talking about."

Dedra continued. "It has a little clown that you cram into a little tin box. The toy has a crank that you tighten and tighten and when the pressure builds up, the clown pops out. The moment when my daughter told me that she had not seen her father, I felt like I had popped to my senses. I felt like enough pressure had finally been exerted to force me out of the can. It was as if my heart had broken free from the spell Keith had put on me. I'd been locked in for so long I didn't know how to get out, or even if it was right to want to get out. But once I was out, I could take á deep breath again. At that moment, he became Keith, a man I once knew. He was no longer Keith, the love of my life, the one for whom I'd do anything. That's when I chose to try to love me as much as I once loved him."

The Chaplain actually smiled at Dedra. It shocked Dedra, because she had never seen her smile. Dedra realized that the Chaplin was very pretty. The Chaplain paused for a minute.

"Dedra, how do you plan to make sure that you never again fall so deeply in love that you lose yourself?"

"I plan to judge a man's actions against his words, to make sure that if he says he loves me, his actions toward me and my children are loving. And I plan to listen to those who really do love me—the people who have stood by me through all of the insanity that has been my life. Now, I realize that my 'love sight' is not 20/20."

Chaplin Denton looked at Dedra and, this time, Dedra saw understanding and compassion.

"Dedra, this is a great place for us to stop today. I appreciate your honesty and thoughtfulness. I'll see you next week."

The rest of Dedra's sessions were insightful. She and the Chaplain talked about her childhood and the patterns that she had inherited from her family. They talked about Dedra's feelings about her sister, whom she believed was prettier and smarter.

"Every year, I'd try out for the cheerleading squad at my school, but I never made it," Dedra recounted. "This was my last chance, I was going to be a senior. So, I read cheerleading books, watched videos and practiced for months. When it was time for try outs, my little sister came to watch. I did great and I was pleased. But, the coach saw my little sister and asked her to try-out. She got up, made up a quick cheer, smiled and flipped her hair. She made the team and I was the alternate. My mom said I should be happy for my sister. But, mom always took up for Greta—every time we got our report cards, she would say I should be more like my sister. And I would work and work and study and study, but I never made all A's like my sister."

Dedra learned about herself, her family and how not to pass her mistakes on to her children. Dedra performed amazingly in the other three program components. A month before she was going to be released, Dedra wrote a long letter to her supervisor at the college where she had worked before going to prison. Her supervisor had left her position at the college to open her own consulting firm and she offered Dedra a job as an executive assistant when she was released.

Greta and Asya attended Dedra's graduation ceremony. They were so proud of her. All of her instructors congratulated her. At the end, the ten graduates ate dinner in the Warden's dining room. Big Lovely served them, and Dedra squeezed her hand as she passed by. Dedra had asked that they consider Big Lovely for the program and she was scheduled for the next class. Big Lovely was ecstatic and Dedra gave her the best advice possible.

"Be honest and accept responsibility for your part in your life's decisions."

After dinner was over and all the tears had been shed and congratulations expressed, Dedra took her little prison-issued bag and left the premises. She had learned her lessons well.

Life on the outside was not going to be easy; she had to get a driver's license and learn her way around again. She not only had to navigate new roads in her city, but also in life as a convicted felon. Whenever she made an application to rent an apartment or a house, the background check always revealed that

Dedra was a convicted felon. She was immediately turned down when she revealed that she had spent almost five years in the State Penitentiary. But, the hardest part about her new freedom was accepting the years she'd missed. She had to get to know her daughter again.

Her new job was marvelous and she was promoted in less than six months. When she applied for custody of Chyna, the Warden's secretary, the Chaplain and her boss spoke on her behalf. In her spare time, Dedra spoke to young girls at the Boys and Girls Club about making good life decisions. She realized she was one of the rare people who had actually been rehabilitated while in prison. Prison had given her a new life that she could be proud of.

Three years after her release, she purchased her first house. It wasn't much, but it had enough room for her and her girls. There was something about the house that reminded her of one of the houses from the magazine photos she had kept in prison. The little house was white with a picture window in front that looked out over a little yard, where several different kinds of rose bushes were planted. Inside, the hardwood floors needed finishing. Dedra loved to watch as the kids sat in front of the fireplace and did their homework while lying on big overstuffed floor pillows. The three 'shopperteers', as they call themselves, spent weekends painting and wallpapering, looking at home improvement shows and finding bargains at garage sales and flea markets while riding around in the sturdy used car she had bought. She started college, determined to finish her bachelor's degree.

Keith spotted Dedra as she stopped on her way home from school to pick up dinner for the girls. He couldn't believe his eyes: she really looked good. His gravy train with the dentist had ended just as fast as it started. He followed Dedra and watched as she opened the garage to a cute little house on Alberta Street. The next day, he called.

When Dedra answered he said, "Hello love of my life..."

"Who is this?" Dedra asked, not recognizing his voice.

Ignoring her question, Keith continued. "I'm so happy you're out of prison. When I heard you were out, I got a divorce. I only wanted to get married so I could provide a stable home for the girls and get them away from that sister of yours. But, now, since you're out there's no need for that. We can be a family again."

Dedra said . . .

1 .   Dedra should

    A.   Try to forge a relationship with Keith so the girls will know their father.

    B.   Realize that Keith is nothing but trouble and stay away from him.

    C.   Try to find a way for the girls to have a relationship with him that does not include her.

2 .   Dedra should

    A.   Give Keith the benefit of the doubt. She has changed, and maybe he has, too.

    B.   Realize that tigers can't change their stripes.

    C.   Seek a harmonious relationship with him for the girls' sake.

3 .   Dedra should

    A.   Allow Keith visitation rights with the girls whenever he wants.

    B.   Try to get him to terminate all parental rights.

    C.   Get the court to mandate supervised visits, only.

4 .   Dedra should

    A.   Seek to reconcile with Keith, because girls really need a father.

    B.   Cut her losses and decide to raise her kids on her own.

    C.   Have him served for child support.

5 .   Dedra should
    A.   Forgive Keith: it was her decision to lie.
    B.   Realize that Keith manipulated and abused her and vow to make sure it doesn't happen again.
    C.   Make sure he is a closed chapter in her life.

6 .   Dedra should
    A.   Listen to his side of the story and let him tell her if he was innocent or guilty.
    B.   Accept her contribution to the problem and move on.
    C.   Try to get the case re-opened.

7 .   What Keith has done in the past
    A.   Has nothing to do with his love for Dedra and their children.
    B.   Has everything to do with who he is now.
    C.   Should require that he be punished.

8 .   Dedra should
    A.   Keep Keith's past from the girls.
    B.   Sit down and explain both her past and Keith's past to the girls in a way that they can understand.
    C.   Make sure they know that Keith is the bad guy.

9 .   Dedra should

A.   Realize that Keith doesn't have a problem; he is a victim of the system.

B.   Help Keith get some help so he can be a better father to the girls.

C.   Stay as far away from Keith as possible.

10 . Dedra should
A.   Continue to play hard to get.
B.   Pack up and move to get away from Keith
C.   Let the police know she is being harassed.

11 . Dedra should
A.   Ignore anything that Greta has to say, because she doesn't understand.
B.   Use her sister as a gauge and a sounding board to make sure she is on the right track.
C.   Take Greta's advice about Keith.

12 . Dedra should consider Keith
A.   A part of her future.
B.   A part of her past that can't be forgotten.
C.   A distant memory.

If your answers total
    Mostly A's read ending X
    Mostly B's read ending Y
    Mostly C's read ending Z

Ending X

"Excuse me, but where did you get my phone number?"

"Baby, your phone number is etched in my heart."

Keith didn't want to tell her that he had gotten her phone number from a phone bill he'd stolen from her mailbox. Keith had parked down the street and watched as Dedra left for work that morning. He wanted to make sure she didn't have a new man. Twice, Dedra's neighbors had knocked on his car window, wanting to give him a jump or help him with his car trouble. It took him ten minutes to explain to Mr. Johnson that he was all right: he was just waiting because the car had overheated and was waiting for it to cool off. Mr. Johnson had felt the neighborly thing to do was to keep him company. Keith refused to let him get a chain to tow the car with his pick-up truck to the Firestone Repair Shop. Mr. Johnson reminded Keith of how nosy the neighbors were on Apple Valley Court.

"I beg your pardon! You certainly have a lot of nerve calling me," Dedra said.

Dedra was trying hard to be mad at Keith, but her emotions were running the gamut: she was upset about the five years she'd spent in jail and his neglect, but she could feel the overwhelming desire to be with him building inside her. It was sending impulses and memories faster than she could process; each one piercing the flimsy armor around her heart.

She remembered the first time she had seen him playing ball with her cousin. He was wearing an old Grateful Dead tee shirt with a navy blue sweatband on his head. What he lacked in ball handling skills, he certainly made up for in the looks department. Dedra also remembered the first time she spoke to him; he had dismissed her like a bad penny. She thought of the first time he made love to her, and how she had felt every nerve cell stand on end. Dedra had convinced herself that all of those thoughts and feelings had been deleted from her memory banks, but in that moment, she realized they had only been misfiled.

Keith's voice brought her back to reality. Her heart was jumping for joy in spite of her good sense. Keith could hear her voice soften.

"Baby," Keith said. "I know I have some explaining to do. I'd rather look in your eyes and tell you than talk over this damned phone."

Dedra, trying to control her oscillating thoughts, said, "Keith, whatever you want to say to me, say it now… because I don't want to see you. I have washed my hands of you."

Keith could tell there was no truth to that statement. He knew full well that she didn't mean it, but he also knew he'd have to tread slowly. He began to weave the backdrop for the story that was still formulating in his head.

"Dedra, I know you've been through a lot because of me. I understand that you were hurt when I didn't visit, but I didn't want to see you so sad. I only wanted us to be happy, but it's as if someone is out to get me. I thought I had brought you so much pain that you would hate me. I didn't want you to hate me, and I couldn't face losing you. I was very, very depressed without you. I even thought of taking my life. But, I just prayed that one day I'd see you again and you'd forgive me. I know it'll take some time, but I'm just praying to the Good Lord that you will."

Dedra felt her resolve melt away. "If you were thinking about me, then who was that woman you married?" she asked.

"I don't know why I did that. I was just lonely. But, I didn't love her. I wanted to see if I could make a home with her so I could have a place to bring Asya . . ."

Dedra interrupted him, "and Chyna."

"Who?"

"Your eight year-old daughter, Chyna…whom you've never seen."

"Yeah. I wanted to get her and Asya away from that sister of yours. But, the court said I needed to have a stable environment and a stepmother for her, for the things girls needed to know—but just until you got out. So, I met someone I thought was nice, but it turned out that she was too selfish to be around my kids."

It all sounded reasonable to Dedra, but she wanted to play a little hardball.

"Let me come over, Dedra. I want to see you and my girls."

"No way. I have to go now."

She hung up the phone and finished washing her dishes. She went to bed and tried to think of something other than Keith. But, that old familiar desire for him had returned. He was the only man who had given her the kind of pleasure that made her want to run and tell the world about her man.

The next day, Dedra was surprised when the delivery man knocked on her office door. She couldn't see his face, which was hidden behind the beautiful roses that he was carrying. She quickly signed for the flowers and tore the envelope open so fast that she tore the card as well. It read, "One Love, One Life, One You. Love. Keith." She smiled and blushed as her co-workers admired the beautiful blossoms that perfumed her office.

Keith waited two days before he called. He could tell by her voice that she was softening.

"Hey Baby, did you get my flowers?"

"Yes, Keith. They are lovely."

"Well, I tried to find something as beautiful as you, but that was impossible, so, I settled for flowers."

He heard the blush in her voice and decided to lay it on a little deep.

"I got some tickets for the circus Saturday night. I thought the four of us could go check it out."

"No, I don't think so."

Keith started begging, repeating lines from the first movie they had seen together.

"Please, baby, please baby, baby, baby, please."

Dedra laughed in spite of her attempt to be cold.

"Okay. Okay. I'm sure the girls would like that."

"It's a date then, I'll pick you up at six. Afterwards, we could have some dinner somewhere."

"Okay."

They had a wonderful time. Keith did all the right things and doted on his girls. Dedra enjoyed seeing the girls play with their father. She thought, *Finally, we can all be a family.* It was as though the last eight years had not happened. Dedra's life was going to be the way she had always dreamed.

Greta realized that it had been a couple of days since she'd talked to her sister. She decided to stop by Dedra's house to tell her the good news in person: Greta had passed her nursing boards. When Greta arrived, she wondered where everybody was. She used her key and entered the dark house. She walked from room to room, looking for clues as to where her sister and the girls might be. She decided to wait. She'd brought margarita mix so Dedra could help her celebrate.

Greta realized she had fallen asleep when a light came on in the darkened room. She thought she had to be dreaming: surely she didn't see Keith in her sister's house. Keith was polite, when he attempted to talk to Greta. Greta had no interest in being civil. She walked out, headed for the kitchen and stayed there until she heard his car pull away.

Dedra knew what was coming. She walked into the kitchen, trying to hide the joy she felt in her soul. She knew that she would have to face the music with her little sister.

"That was pretty rude of you," Dedra said.

"I can accept rude if you can accept, stupid, ignorant, and crazy! Dedra, what the hell is wrong with you? Why was he here?"

Greta's face was tight and ready for the fight.

"He was here because he wanted to spend some time with his girls. He took us all to the circus. Is that a crime? Because if it is, I didn't get the memo."

Greta stared at her, unable to believe her eyes, ears or any of her senses. There was no controlling herself.

"Dedra, are you totally gone in the head? Do you remember that this is the man who beat you for breakfast, lunch and dinner? You spent five years in prison because of him and never once did he set foot in there to see you. In five years, he gave his daughter one twenty-dollar bill and got married to another woman. All while you were doing time because you were trying to save his ass! Did you forget?"

"No, I didn't forget, but I was at fault just as much as Keith was. I prayed, and God said to forgive him."

"Don't you lie on God? God has nothing to do with this. That man is the work of the Devil and anything he touches will go to hell."

"Greta, you just don't understand. He has changed. He is so gentle and loving, you wouldn't believe it."

Shaking her head, Greta said, "You're right about that, Dedra. I wouldn't believe it, and neither should you. If he is 'so loving,' why hasn't he loved you or the kids before now?"

"I am not going to live in the past, Greta. The past is gone and this is now. Now, I have two kids that I have to raise and he is their father."

"No, Dedra. He is not their father. A father takes care of his children and nurtures them. Those kids don't even know him. Dedra he is not a father. He is a sperm donor."

Dedra sat down at the table as her sister paced the floor.

"Greta, I love you. You're my only sister, and I appreciate everything you've done for me. However, this is my life, and you can't control it. I'm a grown woman—"

"Then, why the hell don't you act like a grown woman and stop living in a "Little House on the Prairie" fantasy world? Look at what you've accomplished without him! Look at your life and your kids…he's only going to bring you down. I promise you, everything is going to turn to shit if you let him back in your life."

"Well, that is my decision, and, as for now, I want the girls to get to know their father. If you will excuse me, I've had a long day and I'm going to bed."

Greta grabbed her purse and went out the side door. By the time she reached her car, her sobs were out of control. She sat in her car, parked on the driveway, weeping for her sister and her nieces.

Word of Keith's return spread like wildfire. Everyone tried to talk to Dedra, but she accused them all of trying to ruin her life. Dedra didn't fair very well against Keith's turn on the charm agenda. Within three weeks, he was back in her life and her bed. Things were great: he was kind and considerate and seemed to be devoted to his family. Life was like a fairytale for Dedra and her girls.

Keith couldn't take his eyes off of Asya. She was a pretty girl with long brown hair, kissed red by the sun. She was so pretty and athletic, she had an ass that he could hardly keep himself from touching and her blossoming breasts were the subject of many of his fantasies. Her mouth was quick, and he was determined to tame it. He sent her to her room for getting smart. She refused to go, and he decided to spank her teenaged bottom. But the spanking turned sensual, and Keith had to fight to control himself. Asya recognized the look in his eye: she'd seen it in the faces of teenage boys and even a few of her teachers. She became sullen and withdrawn. Keith tried to draw her out by buying her whatever he could imagine she might want. But Asya seemed to withdraw even more. She saw him watching her, and he had *mistakenly* come into the bathroom while she was showering too many times, even though she was sure she'd locked the door. He always found a reason to rub up against her. She tried to stay out of his way and kept him away from her Chyna, who adored him.

*****

Greta half-heartedly listened to her phone messages as she sorted through the stack of mail on the table, but perked up when she heard the message from Asya's counselor. Greta took down the counselor's number and looked at her watch, hoping she'd catch Mrs. Jeffries before she left school.

Mrs. Jeffries answered the phone and said, "Ms. Donaldson, thank you for returning my call. I wanted to talk to you about Asya. She's been very quiet and sometimes cries in class. I was wondering whether anything was going on at home that would cause her to be depressed."

"I'm not sure. I'm her aunt. But, I'll speak to my sister."

"I'm sorry, I thought you were her mother."

"I was her legal guardian for several years, but now, Asya is back with my sister. However, I will investigate your concerns. I'll come by the school to talk with you as soon as I look into the matter."

Greta hung up the phone and immediately began dialing her sister's number, but hung up before it rang. She knew that nothing would be resolved if she spoke to Dedra, so she decided to take matters into her own hands. She walked out onto the balcony of her apartment and watched the cars until a plan started to form in her mind.

Greta was sitting outside the school when Asya got off the bus. She had taken the day off and told her niece that the two of them were going to have a 'cut day' so they could hang out together. Greta knew when Asya was lying or telling the truth, so she asked Asya outright what was bothering her. It didn't take much for Asya's emotions to spill over. She told her aunt about her dad's inappropriate touches, how he always found a reason to rub against her, and how he had broken the lock on the bathroom door to walk in on her several times. Asya told her aunt about the night he said he was drunk and got into her bed by mistake. He'd left when she screamed for her mother, who came to get him and bought his drunk routine, hook, line and sinker. One night while Dedra was working late, he'd grabbed Asya's breast and tried to kiss her. Since that time, Keith's attempts to touch and fondle her had begun to escalate. Asya began to take "No Doze pills" to keep her awake through the night.

Greta saw red. She took the tape she had secretly made during the conversation with her niece to the police and then, to Dedra at her job. Dedra was convinced that it was all very innocent, but Chaplain Denton's voice came to her mind. *"You lied to protect a pedophile?"* Dedra's fantasy world began to collapse.

She said, "I'll talk to him, I'm sure there is an explanation. He wouldn't do that, Asya is his child."

"Are you dumb, stupid or both? Will a boulder have to drop from the sky for you to see Keith for who he is?" Greta asked.

"I'm not dumb or stupid, I know my man."

Greta called Asya in, and asked her to tell her mom about their conversation. Dedra watched as her daughter spoke, and knew she was telling the truth. Greta supported her as her legs began to go weak.

Dedra went home and packed all of Keith's things, put them on the lawn and called him to come get them. She told him she had contacted the police and that she and Asya would both, testify against him. She warned him never to come near her or her daughters again. She sent Asya and Chyna to stay with Greta while she sold the house, and found a therapist for herself and her daughters.

Ending Y

Dedra held the phone for a second, feeling a rush of emotions. She took a deep breath and in the most polite voice she could muster, said, "Keith, it was so nice of you to call. I've wanted to talk to you for a long time. In fact, while I was in prison, I wrote you letter after letter."

Dedra paused to take another deep breath, exhaling in an angry rush, like opening a vacuum-sealed can. She took several moments to control her emotions and her voice, but the anger won.

"Never mind Keith, all that is not relevant now. It took me a while, but I realize now that you are a sorry excuse for a man…"

"Baby, I know you're mad, but I couldn't bring myself to come to that place. It made me sick to think of it. I really had a hard time, baby. I was in bad shape."

Dedra thought she heard him crying.

"I can understand you being upset," she said. "It was an absolutely horrible place, and I wouldn't wish my worst enemy to a place like that. And, oftentimes, I cried too. But that's behind me now, and so are my feelings for you. Right now, we have two subjects to talk about Asya and Chyna."

Keith thought, *I'm going to have to lay it on heavy and wear her down.*

"Dedra, there is no way you can be through with me. I'm your soul mate and you're mine. God put us together. We belong to each other. I'm sorry I couldn't come to visit you, but seeing you in that place was like seeing a part of me in there."

"And it should have been you in there, not me. But that's my fault. I can't blame it on you. It was all me. I didn't make good decisions."

Just then, Asya walked into the kitchen, got an apple from the fruit bowl, and returned to the den to do her homework. Seeing Asya put everything into perspective for Dedra.

"I can try," Dedra said. "Even though it doesn't make sense, I understand the reason why you didn't visit me in prison, but one thing I don't understand is why you couldn't visit your daughters. Why didn't you even attempt to see them? Why didn't you even remember their birthdays or get them anything for Christmas? If you want to give me that line of bull about not being able to see me in prison, then what is your excuse for not seeing them? They weren't in prison."

"I didn't visit them because I thought it would make things worse for them. I know how your family feels about me. That's no secret, so I stayed away. I thought it was best for them. I couldn't take care of them, so I didn't want to interfere with things and get your folks all riled up."

"You knew they needed food and clothing. Why didn't you at least send some kind of support?"

"Dedra, I wanted to, but it took me a long time to find a job. I was so depressed. You should have seen me. I didn't know what to do."

Dedra was beginning to get bored with the conversation.

"Keith, I can't undo the past and neither can you. I'm not sure I'd want to if I could. I've learned some things and I'm not the stupid little girl you met. I'm a woman with little girls of my own and it happens that my little girls are also your little girls. So, this is how it's going to work. If you want to see your girls, that's fine. I will meet you and allow you to visit with them, but you're too unstable for me to leave them in your care."

"What the hell do you mean? Unstable? They are my fucking children. I will come and get them whenever I like."

"If you like, we can have the family court settle the matter for us. You are welcome to have supervised visits."

"No one is going to supervise me with my own damn kids."

"Keith, I have to help my daughter with her math. I wish I could say it was nice talking to you, but that would be a lie. Have a good evening."

Before he could reply, Dedra hung up the phone and took the receiver off the hook.

*****

Dedra waved when she saw Mr. Johnson from across the street walking Bojangles, his white German Shepherd. Dedra got her briefcase and purse out of the car and let the garage door down behind her. Her face turned to stone when she entered the kitchen and found Chyna sitting on Keith's lap, looking uncomfortable.

"Welcome home, baby. I decided to come see my kids."

Dedra slowly put her things down on the stool next to the wall phone.

"Asya, take your sister to your room. I'll be there in a minute."

Keith smiled his best 'you-can't-resist-all-this' smile. He turned and looked after the girls and said, "Yeah kids, go play for a minute. I need to talk to your mom. We have some catching up to do."

Dedra never took her eyes off of Keith. She didn't address the question in Asya's eyes or the concern in Chyna's. Once the kids were gone, Dedra kicked her blue slingbacks off and pulled out a chair at the table opposite Keith. He was the first to speak.

"Baby, is that all the greeting I get? It's been over seven years since I've seen you. Come, sit on Big Poppa's lap, run your hand in my pocket, and see how glad I am to see you."

"Don't you ever, as long as you live, come to my house or bother my children. If you want to see them, call me and I will arrange it. Obviously, you have my number."

Keith laughed. "Who do you think you're talking to? I'm not some patsy off the street. I will come and go as I please. This house is my house, now."

He stood up over Dedra. In a previous life, the tone Keith was using with her would have sent her running for cover. Dedra let out a little snicker and took her time standing to meet his glance.

Keith didn't understand. There was no fear in her face and her body language was strong and confident. "Sit your ass down, Dedra."

The sound of angry voices brought Chyna and Asya to check on their mother.

"Asya, take your sister to your room and do not come out until I come get you. Do you understand me?" Dedra said.

Asya shook her head as tears rose to her eyes. Dedra's eyes never left Keith's. He walked closer to her, standing only a fraction of an inch away from her, with his hand raised as if he was about to slap her. Dedra could smell the fish and chips he'd had for dinner.

"Sit your ass down, Dedra."

Dedra never changed expressions. "Keith, if you leave now, I will consider letting you live."

When he laughed and pushed her toward the chair, all of Dedra's frustration, anger and resentment came pouring out of her at once. She tucked her head and made contact with his stomach, knocking him into the wall. As he stumbled, she caught him with an uppercut to his nose and five or six quick jabs to his kidney, making him urinate on himself. Keith tried to grab his side, but the blood flowing from his nose seemed to have slowed his responses. Dedra kicked him in his crotch and grabbed the pressure point behind his ear, causing him to scramble to his feet. Dedra began to punch him in the face and stomach. She grabbed an iron skillet from the pot rack above the stove and began to connect with his forearms and legs. She knew the crunch that she heard was the sound of a bone breaking, but she didn't know which one. There was not a part of Keith's body that she did not hit. In less than 300 seconds, Dedra had made him wish he'd stayed home.

Aysa heard the commotion and called 911. The police interrupted the beating of Keith's life when Dedra stopped her attack to answer the door. She explained to the officers what was happening. The ambulance arrived and took Keith away. He looked like he'd been the lone victim of a gang fight. The police were curious as to how Dedra could have beaten him so badly: he outweighed her by at least 70 pounds and was nearly a foot taller. She didn't tell them that five years in prison was all the self-defense class she ever needed. The police gave her permission to call her sister to come stay with the girls before they took her to jail.

Greta arrived in what seemed like seconds, wearing boxer shorts and a terry cloth robe with no shoes. When she saw the scene and an unscathed Dedra, she kissed her handcuffed sister and gave her a knowing hug.

"Don't worry, about a thing. We'll meet you at the jail in a couple of minutes."

Dedra nodded her head, embarrassed that her children had to see her in handcuffs.

The day of the trial, Dedra's defense attorney had the court packed with Dedra supporters—that even included Keith's ex-wife. If found guilty, Dedra's probation could have been revoked. With the stakes so high, her defense attorney was ready to fight like Dedra, to the bitter end. Keith was a no-show; he was too ashamed to show his broken and bruised self to the court. Besides, he had an outstanding warrant for an unpaid traffic ticket. So the case was dismissed and Dedra was allowed to go home with her children.

Dedra left the courthouse wrapped in the arms of her girls. She vowed that she would never let anything happen that could possibly separate them again. She assured both of them that she would never leave them again. Dedra did her best to explain that violence is not the answer, but when a woman's children are in danger, a woman rises to the occasion to protect them.

In the minds of her children, she was a hero. Asya tried to convince her mom to become a boxer and challenge Laila Ali.

Ending Z

"Keith, the number of my case worker at Family Court is 555-2905. If you need to discuss anything in regards to your children, you can contact Ms. Jacobs at 555-2905. She is working on having you served for child support and visitation issues. There is no other reason why you need to call me or make contact with my family."

With that, Dedra wished Keith a good night and hung up.

Keith held onto the phone. This was not the Dedra he knew. What the hell was she talking about? He had to lay low: he didn't make enough money for her to try to get child support from him.

Dedra called the phone company and had her phone number changed. The next phone call was one that she had put off for over a year now. She called the mother of Keith's victim, explained who she was, and apologized for her actions. The girl's mother said she would pass along her message to her daughter. Dedra looked in on her girls as they slept peacefully in their beds. Dedra knelt beside the bed her daughters shared and prayed, thanking God for the blessings she was allowed to come home to. Finally, the prodigal daughter had found her way home and to the self she had been created to be.

Yasmine

It was one of those Saturdays made for hotdogs and cold beer. Yasmine and Ava were hanging out, watching the "two-legged wildlife." The campus was almost empty. The spring semester had ended and summer school had not begun. They talked freely about everything. The two girls couldn't be more different. Yasmine was lean, 5'10" tall, a girlie-girl; make-up and clothes were her passion. She knew all the latest trends in fashion and could spot a knock-off from a block away. Ava was earthy; her normal attire was jeans, a tee-shirt and her tight curls pulled back with a headband. She was short and curvaceous, with a sharp wit and an even sharper intellect. Ava was more into world affairs and politics than fashion, and she loved to shop resale shops for vintage clothing. Yasmine was more traditional. She'd gone to college to find a suitable husband, settle down, have babies and live the country club life. They found themselves on the same side of a debate in a philosophy class, in fact, they were the only two on that side, but in the end, they won.

After the debate, they became fast friends. They had both come from large southern families. Ava had four siblings and Yasmine had six. Yasmine learned early on to depend on her good looks to get ahead. She'd been raised to be charming and lady-like. Five years of charm and finishing school had taught her all the social graces to help her find a man and marry into the right kind of family. Yasmine always remembered her mother's words of caution: Don't marry a poor man for love and have to wonder how your children will be fed. Ava's mother was a civil rights attorney who believed in the liberation of all minorities, including women. Ava had been taught to be independent and self sufficient.

Ava sat Indian style with her legs folded beneath her as if she were about to perform some ancient ceremony. Yasmine sat perfectly erect with her legs to the side. Each girl was holding an envelope.

"Yasie, you will be moving to Dallas, Texas. Your internship is with the FBI."

"Damn, the FBI was my last choice. Wow, I didn't expect that. I really wanted New York, DC or Chicago. I don't know anything about being a cowgirl."

Ava's eyes filled with tears. She said, "I'm going to miss you Yasie."

"You don't know. You might be going with me."

"I know I won't because I didn't apply to the FBI," Ava said, wiping her eyes.

Yasmine looked sad. This was the closest friendship she had ever had. The girls in high school had treated her badly because she was too pretty and the other girls didn't want to compete with her. No one seemed to understand her--until she met Ava. They seemed to be able to read each other's minds.

"Okay, I'm ready! Tell me where I'm going to spend the next year of my life."

Yasmine took the envelope and began to open it in slow motion.

"Yasie, open the damn thing," barked Ava.

Yasmine gave the envelope one big rip and started to read the letter in a very official tone. "This letter comes to you from Louisiana State University. It is dated May 3, 1985."

"Don't play with me Yasie!"

Yasmine looked at Ava with a very sad expression on her face.

"Oh no," said Ava, putting her face in her hands. "Don't tell me I didn't get an internship at all. Damn, I'll have to see if they will hire me at Wal-Mart for the summer."

Ava tried to snatch the letter from her friend, but Yasmine got up and ran with it.

"Yasie, I'm not playing with you. When I catch you I'm going to rip the hair out of your head and break all your Rod Stewart records."

Yasmine, laughing said, "In that case I better not let you catch me."

Yasmine ran back to the blanket and said, "Okay okay, I'm tired. I'll tell you! You're going to Dallas, Texas where you'll work for the Internal Revenue Service."

Both girls jumped around, holding each other. They really wanted to be together and had planned on getting an apartment together.

The next week was a blur. The girls packed their meager belongings and pooled their money to buy a torn up Volvo from one of their classmates who was graduating and going to work overseas in the Peace Corp. They were so excited that they would be working in the same building. They could ride to work together and eat lunch together and sneak out for breaks together.

They found a reasonable apartment, not too far from work, and furnished it with band posters, bean bag chairs and whatever they could round up at the re-sale shops and the Salvation Army. The girls were ecstatic, they were so proud of their first apartment.

Orientation was hectic; the girls were trying to learn procedures, practices, names and the politics in their offices. Ava's assignment at the IRS was humdrum; she learned forms, exemptions, and audit techniques. After a week, she was completely bored with the job, and wondered how she would manage a whole year. Yasmine was learning exciting things that she came home and told her roommate about: surveillance, covert missions, phone taps, self-defense, defensive driving, lie detector testing, and body language. She was so excited; it was contagious. Ava looked forward to what Yasie learned each day.

Yasmine had been on the job about a month when she was sent to have a psychological evaluation. She didn't know what to expect, but someone should have warned her that the psychiatrist was a drop-dead gorgeous hunk of a man. He had lashes long enough to braid, deep-set dimples, and a perfect complexion. He was 6'3" well built; even through his suit, she could tell that he had muscles in all the right places. His hair was coal black with a slight wave. He looked like he could be a GQ model, with manicured nails, an expertly tailored Armani suit, a custom made shirt with initials on the cuffs, and Italian leather shoes. Everything about him was flawless except for the scar above his left eyebrow, a remnant from his college football days. He was the most beautiful man Yasmine had seen in all her twenty-one years of living.

He waved her to a seat, but she stood, staring at him and not hearing him ask her to sit down. She thought if she took her eyes off of him he would disappear. She felt like one of those girls who were star struck over a rock star. He didn't look amused. It appeared that he was used to women behave that way around him. Yasmine had done a quick search on him before her appointment, and she'd discovered that he had been the star running back at UCLA, but had chosen medical school over the football contract from the New York Jets to follow in his dad's footsteps. In an interview he quoted his dad as saying, "Football is a temporary career, but medicine is a lifelong career." Yasmine noticed that his football trophies were the only personal items in his office. She wondered how he could have given up the glamorous life of the NFL with its multi-million dollar salary and all the fame. Being a doctor was great, but a professional in the NFL -- now that was what dreams were made of.

"I am Dr. Thaddeus Morgan," he said. "And I have been asked to give you a battery of psychological tests for the Bureau to determine your strengths and weakness, problem solving skills and how you would most likely perform under stress . . ."

Yasmine heard every third word or so, she couldn't take her eyes off of this gorgeous man.

"Miss Hunter, do you understand what I have just told you?"

Yasmine tried to snap back. "No doctor, could you repeat that?"

Dr. Morgan repeated his spiel in a very matter of fact and somewhat irritated manner.

Yasmine willed herself to listen. She expressed her understanding of the process, and signed the consent documents.

For the next several hours, she chose words from a list, looked at inkblots, completed statements and selected answers from multiple possibilities. She was shown crime scene pictures and asked to identify evidence. It was quite exciting, but not nearly as exciting as the man who was administering the test. He only spoke when he gave instructions, and seemed annoyed by her presence. It was as if she were keeping him from some great task that would save the world.

The morning went by very fast. Yasmine soaked up the doctor's scent, knowing she would need it for the fantasies he was beginning to create in her mind. But, Dr. Morgan did not seem to notice.

He said, "Miss Hunter, we will break for lunch now, and I'll see you again this afternoon, at one-thirty."

"You can call me Yasmine . . ."

"No, Ms. Hunter, I prefer to call you by your given surname." He strolled to the door, opened it for her, and then said, "One-thirty, Ms. Hunter."

Yasmine was waiting outside of her office when Ava appeared with two of her co-workers, headed for lunch. Yasmine pounced on her. Ava could tell something had happened because Yasie was wearing her 'you won't believe what just happened' look on her face. Ava told her friends that she would catch up later, while Yasmine went on and on in her animated fashion, telling Ava about her session with Dr. Morgan. She told her friend everything about him—down to the Calvin Klein socks he was wearing.

She finished her dissertation with, "I know he is the one. He's the man I'm going to marry, he's going to be my husband."

Ava was stunned; she had never seen her friend like this before. Usually men fell all over Yasmine and she critiqued them harshly, looking for someone who her mother would approve of.

The girls never made it to lunch. They sat on the bench in the ladies room while Yasmine recounted her morning to Ava. Ava listened very carefully and warned her friend not to jump in with both feet. Yasmine didn't even know if he was married.

"Yasmine," Ava reasoned. "It seems that you are just interested in this man because he's a doctor and because he's good looking. What about his character and all the other important things? Those things take time, you've known him for less than four hours and you're already making the guest list for the wedding. What do you know about him, other than he's a psychiatrist? From what you've said he seems a little shallow and insensitive."

"We'll have the rest of our lives to work on all of that. For now you have to come with me this evening to buy some new clothes and some sexy underwear."

Observing the look in her friend's eyes, Ava said, "Yasie, slow down. What if he's in a relationship with someone—or God forbid, married?"

"Then you'll have to help me hide her body."

This time both girls laughed.

Ava went back to her office and Yasmine went back to her afternoon session. She arrived at one-fifteen and saw Dr. Morgan in the corridor ahead of her. She rushed to catch up with him. As he opened the door to his office, he said, "Ms. Hunter, I will see you at one-thirty and then he closed the door in her face.

At one-thirty on the dot, Dr. Morgan emerged from the office and opened the door for Yasmine, who could not help but grin at the sight of him. As soon as Yasmine finished the afternoon test, she asked, Dr. Morgan how she had done.

"Miss Hunter," said Dr. Morgan in a sterile tone, "I will not be able to provide you with that information until the instruments are properly calibrated. Upon completion of that task, your unit chief will be provided with a report, and you are entitled to a copy. He will advise you from that point. Good day, Miss Hunter."

With that, he swung the door open for Yasmine to exit. On the way out, Yasmine pivoted and leaned against the open door, trying to strike a seductive pose. When his expression didn't change, she asked, "Dr. Morgan you have a very distinctive accent. I can't quite catch it. Can you tell me where you're from?"

"I'm sorry Ms. Hunter, but I do not discuss matters regarding my personal life."

Dr. Morgan gently took her elbow and guided her out of his office and into the corridor, and with a dry smile, he bid her good day again and closed the door.

Ava rolled her eyes as Yasmine came out of the dressing room wearing a bright yellow strapless dress with a handkerchief hem.

"Yasie, the only place you see this man is at work. Shouldn't you buy something for work? Anyway, how are you going to afford all of this?"

"Well roomie, sister, friend, I was thinking maybe, you could lend me some money until my next pay day," Yasmine said, biting her finger and batting her eyes.

"Next pay day you still won't be able to afford all of this. I thought we were going to save money for books and school and the vacation we were going to take."

"I know, I know, but please do this for me," Yasmine begged, gazing upward dreamily. "You should see his eyes."

Ava, rolling her eyes, said, "Yasie, you've known this man less than twelve hours and already you're obsessed with him. And from what you've told me, he has NO interest in you. I can't let you go out like this. Pull yourself together. Buy one outfit--one that you can wear to work, so it won't be such a waste of money."

"I can't wear the same outfit every day, I have to look nice."

"Yasie, could it be that you are just going through all of this because he ignored you? You're just not used to having men ignore you. They usually fall out over you and you can't stand it because he doesn't. Could it be that you want him because he doesn't seem to want you?"

Yasmine gathered herself before she screamed at her roommate, "No, Ava! I want him because I know he is the man for me. I just know it. He's tall, he's good-looking, and he's a doctor. My mom told me to marry a doctor."

"But, what if he doesn't want to marry you? What if he has someone else? What if he is already married?"

Yasmine didn't answer. It was a feeling that Yasie couldn't put into words. Ava watched Yasmine carefully, knowing that her mind was already made up, and there was no changing it. Ava helped Yasie load the boxes and bags from her shopping spree into the trunk of the car.

Ava shook her head. "Do you realize you have just spent more than one month's salary?"

"Yeah, we really got some good bargains and it will be worth more than that when the good Dr. Morgan does a double take when he sees me."

*****

"Damn, when does the good doctor come to work?" Yasmine muttered to herself. I've been waiting here for almost an hour with no sign of him. The guard's been watching me for the last fifteen minutes."

Yasmine reluctantly went to her office; her mind was spinning with thoughts of Dr. Thaddeus Morgan. When the casual meeting she'd planned in the lobby didn't work out, Yasmine started to formulate another plan to be in his company. Since she had already planned their wedding and decided what their children were going to look like, the only thing left was to find an entry into his world. She took a chance and called his office.

He answered on the first ring. "Hello, this is Dr. Morgan."

"Yes, Dr. Morgan, this is Yasmine Hunter. I have a few questions about the test I took yesterday."

"Yes, Miss Hunter. How can I help you?"

"I was wondering, which test is designed to measure what?"

"Miss Hunter, the psychological instruments are not meant to be taken singularly, but collectively. All the various instruments provide a piece of the puzzle that can only be properly analyzed when appraised communally."

"I find that fascinating. I'd love to discuss it with you, perhaps over lunch?"

"Miss Hunter, I'm afraid that is all I can tell you about the psychological instruments used by the Bureau. Perhaps you should discuss the process with your unit chief, he might be helpful to you."

"Well, maybe you could share more details about the fascinating work you do?"

"Miss Hunter, I have an appointment. I do hope the rest of your day is pleasant."

Yasmine held the receiver in her hand and listened to the dial tone for a minute. She was not deterred, but maybe the direct approach wasn't right. Maybe, her unit chief was the answer.

Charlie was the nice guy who women automatically put in the friend category. He was never taken seriously, even though he was a great friend: sensitive, giving and dedicated. He had given up on romance, so he had dedicated his life to the Bureau. He was an excellent trainer because he was so easy to trust. He watched as the women around him chose the wrong men and come to cry on his shoulders. He had come to grips with his lot in life. He was attractive, but didn't have that air of mystery that attracted women. Most women considered him a little too eager. He was the kind of man who was so nice and predictable that he wasn't a challenge.

Yasmine decided to start Plan C with Charlie. He would be easy. She'd noticed his eyes linger on her a few seconds too long when she was near. He liked to pat her hand or shoulder when they talked. Yasmine knew Dr. Morgan would become her most important covert mission. But, first, she'd have to make sure Charlie was on board. Yasmine entered his office early the next morning.

"Hey Charlie," she said smiling widely. "How are you today? I wanted to thank you for the tips on the range the other day, so I made some brownies. You aren't allergic are you?"

Charlie knew instantly that the brownies weren't free, they had some price attached, and he didn't know whether he was willing to pay it or not.

He thought for a minute and then said, "No, I'm not allergic, I love chocolate."

"Which would you like? Nuts or without nuts or nuts and caramel?" Yasmine, smiled as she revealed the assortment of goodies. Her mother had taken great pains to teach her to cook; telling her that cooking was a very powerful tool that a woman should know how to use, in order to get what she wants.

"What's the real occasion, Yasmine?" Charlie asked, still eyeing the plate of goodies.

"No occasion. I just felt like baking and I wanted to thank you for helping me, so I put the two together and here goes. But, if we really need a reason to celebrate, I guess we could celebrate my almost two month anniversary at the Bureau."

"Well, I think that's worthy of celebrating. I'll take the caramel nut brownie."

"Oh, Charlie, take one of each. You can have one with your coffee and one with your lunch and one because I've watched you working out in the gym and all those muscles need feeding."

Charlie agreed, glad that someone had noticed his muscles. He took the small paper plate and napkin Yasmine handed to him. He started to ask, but knew instinctively that the price was about to come front and center. Yasmine watched as he licked the gooey mess from fingers.

"Very good, very good. Beauty, brains, and a good cook too. What a combination."

Yasmine smiled. Charlie waited to find out what she wanted.

After a few seconds, Yasmine said, "You know Charlie, I was wondering about all the tests that Dr. Morgan gave me a couple of days ago. What are they designed to measure exactly?"

The clue was in the inflection on his name. Charlie thought, *So she has the Dr. Morgan fever. Wow. What do all the women see in that prick? He doesn't even have a personality.*

Charlie answered Yasmine's question rather than deal with the implied questions.

"The test provides a profile that will help the bureau place different agents on assignments. They provide an indication of how you would perform under pressure, whether you're sure of yourself, whether you will doubt your instincts at critical moments, whether you are likely to see evidence or overlook tiny details, how quickly you can access a situation and decide on a course of action. Also, the test gives an indication of where we need to focus training for individual agents."

"Wow, that's really interesting. Have you gotten my results back yet?"

"No, I haven't. They'll be back before the end of the week. Why? Are you so anxious? It's not like you can fail these tests?"

"I know. I'm just curious about my scores and where I'll best fit in the Bureau."

Charlie took another bite of his brownie. "My dear, the sky is the limit when it comes to you. You can have a wonderful career here. In fact, the bureau does not test anyone unless they think they have the aptitude to succeed. You've worked out very well and I'm sure the bureau will make you a job offer to consider after your graduation. Don't you worry, you did just fine."

Yasmine smiled her 'Little ole Southern Bell Smile' that usually opened doors for her with men and women alike.

"Thanks, Charlie. That means a lot, coming from someone like you. Now, speaking of great careers: where do we start today?"

Charlie looked at the assignment sheets. "Today you're going to learn how to develop a surveillance plan. You'll be working with Pam and Steve in lab three."

Yasmine thought, *Surveillance plan, that's what I need.*

*****

I can't believe Ava wouldn't come with me. She's getting too serious, just like those other IRS nerds, Yasmine thought. Yasmine thought of Ava at home in those thick multi colored socks with the toes in them. She understood why she couldn't come, but she missed her still. The Dallas heat in August was almost too much for Yasmine, as she sat in her rented car and watched Dr. Morgan's house. This was the third night in a row and he hadn't gone out.

He always stopped at the same restaurant for takeout and beer. After eating a bag of popcorn, two candy bars, a banana and a cup of yogurt, Yasmine was thinking about leaving. Her clothes were sticking to her and she was tired. Maybe this wasn't a good idea, after all. She was just about to pull away from the curb when a shiny black SAAB began to back out of the garage.

"Yes, we're on the move," Yasmine squealed.

She followed Dr. Morgan to the restaurant at the Ritz Carlton Hotel, where a stylish older woman wearing Vera Wang was waiting for him. Then a man, who looked like an older version of Dr. Morgan, came from the bar, holding two glasses of wine. They greeted each other with a handshake and Dr. Morgan seemed nervous. He looked to the woman, who patted the seat next to her for him to sit down.

Yasmine laughed and said, "Well, it's nice to finally meet my future in-laws."

She watched until the maître d' came to seat them for dinner, then drove back to Dr. Morgan's house, parked down the street and walked up to the small bungalow. She checked the windows for contact seals, identified the type of system and disarmed it. She walked through the small house. It was immaculate. All the shoes in the closet were in a perfectly shined row. All of the hangers in the closet were one-eighth of an inch apart. His shirts started from white then went progressively to the darker colors. All were monogrammed. His suits were sorted from black to gray getting increasingly lighter down the line. The pinstriped suits were in a section of their own. His slippers sat neatly by the bed and the bathroom looked as if he scrubbed it with a toothbrush: no shower scum, no toothpaste specks on the mirror, and no ring around the tub. The refrigerator was neat and clean, possessing orange juice, bottled water, beer, eggs, raisin bread and salad fixings in the crisper. Yasmine looked for dust, but found none.

She looked at her watch; she had to hurry. She hastily placed the bug in his phone and a small camera in his bedroom where the pleats in the curtains met. It was almost ten o'clock. Yasmine finished her work and tried to cover her tracks. She reconnected the security system and made it back to the Ritz Carlton just in time to see him kiss the middle-aged well-dressed woman, whom she recognized as his mother from the photos in his house.

Ava looked up from the television as Yasmine came through the door. "If it isn't I SPY. When are you going to leave that man alone?"

Yasmine walked past Ava and went to the refrigerator. "I'll never leave him alone."

Ava leaned over the kitchen breakfast bar and said, "Yasie, I think you need to get some help, it's not natural for you to be so obsessed with this man. He's shown no interest in you. He's turned you down at least fifty times, for lunch, dinner, parties, picnics, movies. Don't you think it's time for you to move on? Honey it's been months and he's not interested."

Ava, noticing Yasmine's tears, spoke very softly, "Yasie, I'm worried about you. This is not you. I don't know this woman that you're turning into."

"Ava, you just don't understand. You're different from me. You're stronger than me. I can't explain it. I love him and that's all I know!"

"Yasie, make me understand. You're my best friend and I love you. We're not that different--up until a couple of months ago we understood everything about each other. Explain to me what's going on with you. I don't want to ridicule you. I want to understand."

"Ava, I love him, I just love him. I can't explain it. It's as if he is the other half of my soul. I know he's the one, but he just hasn't realized it yet."

"Yasie you can't keep following him and breaking into his house. You're going to have to get over this. I know it's hard. Remember when I was so in love with Tony? I felt as if my heart was going to dissolve in my chest, but I got through it. You helped me through it and it took a while, but I got over him. Let me help you find a way to get over him, Yasie. You can't go on living like this. It's just not healthy."

"I don't need help trying to get over him. I need help finding a way into his life."

"Yasie! He has refused every advance you've made. And even though you think he's the one, he has to believe it too. You can't make him want you. Remember that song you like by Bonnie Raitt? It says, 'You can't make his heart do what it won't.' And Sweetie, if you just open your eyes, you will find someone who will love you like you love him."

"It's not the same," Yasmine said, walking away.

*****

"Charlie did you need to see me?"

Charlie put down the telephone handset and turned to face Yasmine.

"Close the door and have a seat, please."

Yasmine sat on the edge of her seat, wondering what this was all about.

Charlie took a minute and sized her up before he asked, "Yasmine, can you give me any good reason why you have Dr. Morgan under surveillance?"

Yasmine felt as if the wind had been knocked out of her.

"I don't have him under surveillance. What gave him a stupid idea like that?"

"Every time a search is pulled on an employee of the bureau, I get a report. I received a report that you pulled a background report on Dr. Morgan. This morning, Dr. Morgan came to my office and showed me a bureau-issued bug that had been placed in his house. When we checked access, the computer flagged you."

Yasmine was trying not to look guilty. She'd have to find a way out of this one and she wasn't sure how she'd manage it.

Yasmine's actions were cause for termination, but Charlie wanted to give her the benefit of the doubt, even though he had no doubt.

"Dr. Morgan thought he was being followed and found it interesting that he later saw you at the Ritz Carlton. I told him that there had to be an explanation." Charlie came from behind his desk and sat in the chair next to Yasmine. "You have a great future here and I'd like to know why are you jeopardizing your future by performing an unauthorized investigation of Dr. Morgan."

Yasmine took a deep breath and said, "Charlie, I was just curious about the guy and decided to put some of the techniques I am learning into practice. I don't know very many people in Dallas, so I felt like he was an easy target--especially since he is such a prick."

Charlie hid his amusement. On that point, they agreed. But for some reason, he knew the story was deeper than that.

"I'm glad you want to hone your skills, but you cannot make unauthorized investigations. You are to discontinue any attempts to follow Dr. Morgan and refrain from going to his residence or making any contact with him whatsoever. Do you understand me?"

"Yes sir, I do. I want to apologize for my behavior."

"If you want to go on surveillance, talk to Gene. He is working a case you might find interesting."

Yasmine thanked Charlie and left his office. What was she going to do?

I can't follow him anymore. I guess it's time for plan D, Yasmine thought.

*****

When Dr. Morgan arrived at the hospital fund raiser he was shocked to see Yasmine seated next to his mother.

"Darling, I'd like you to meet Ms. Hunter," his mother said. "She has been so helpful to me over the last few months and, you won't believe it. She works in your building, Dear. Isn't it a small world?"

Dr. Morgan managed a polite hello. His mother insisted that he sit next to Yasmine, who was so happy that she could have burst.

"Darling, the two of you look perfect together. Ms. Hunter is a very interesting young lady, as I'm sure you'll discover when you get to know her. I've invited her to come with us to the Vineyard, for the weekend."

"Mother, I'm sure Ms. Hunter has plans of her own."

"Oh no, Dr. Morgan. I'm completely free, as I told your mother. I'm looking forward to the trip." Yasmine smiled softly at Mrs. Morgan.

"I thought you two young people might want to spend some time there and get acquainted. You work much too hard and now its time for you to pay attention to your social life. You aren't getting any younger."

Over the next several months, Yasmine sought Mrs. Morgan's advice about everything. She became the daughter Mrs. Morgan never had. They shopped together, tried the same beauty products, and even got their nails done in the same color. The two women talked for hours on the phone. Yasmine shared her background, confessing how much she wanted to overcome her meager beginnings. Mrs. Morgan appreciated Yasmine's honesty and she understood because she too had climbed the social ladder and married well.

Who knew the way to get to Dr. Morgan was through his mother? Dr. Morgan loved seeing his mother more active and happy. He was thankful to Yasmine for that. She could tell by the way he looked at her that he only tolerated her for his mother's sake. He never said two words to her or paid any attention to her if they were alone. Mrs. Morgan had practically begged her son to marry Yasmine, telling him it was time. She said she wanted to see him married before she died.

When he finally proposed, he gave Yasmine his grandmother's ring. Yasmine wasn't happy about the pre-nup she had to sign, but she was getting the man, and that was what truly mattered. His mother was ecstatic; she used the wedding as an opportunity to impress all her friends.

Ava begged Yasmine not to marry Dr. Morgan. She said, "Yasie, why would you do this, when he told you that he doesn't love you? His mother does. Why would you want a man who doesn't love you? Yasie, he already told you that the only reason he is marrying you is because his mother asked him to, and he has never disobeyed his mother. What kind of life will that be for you?"

"I'll make him love me."

"Yasie, you can't make him love you. I keep telling you that, but you won't listen. Don't you want to be happily married?"

On a beautiful Saturday morning one year after her junior year internship had ended and a week after college graduation, Yasmine and Thaddeus Morgan were married. Yasmine was blissfully happy. It was a beautiful wedding. Mrs. Morgan was almost as happy as Yasmine. She'd spent a fortune on the wedding and had planned every detail. Ava cried through the whole ceremony. Some people thought she was moved by the beauty of it all; others thought she was crying because the bridesmaid's dresses were so ugly.

All the wedding pictures showed a sullen looking groom with a sad smile on his face and a bride who was grinning all over herself. Yasmine's mother was so pleased. Three months after the wedding, Thaddeus and Yasmine consummated their marriage. Thaddeus didn't want Yasmine to tell his mother that they had a sexless marriage, so he gave in to her pressure. It was a performance that left Yasmine begging for more. Thaddeus seemed unmoved and immediately got up to shower.

Everyone at the Bureau thought they were the perfect couple, two beautiful people who had found each other. Yasmine loved to go out with her husband, and in public, he treated her like a fragile China doll. At home there were days and days where he would not speak. Sex was infrequent and unfulfilling, regardless of what she tried. She'd asked him to go to a sex therapist, but he'd laughed in her face. Every once in awhile he'd respond to her advances, but she could tell there was someone else on his mind. He'd have sex with her, but he would never kiss her.

Yasmine busied herself with shopping with her mother-in-law to furnish their new house. Yasmine had a great eye, but usually conceded to his mother's selections. After the house was finished, Yasmine had too much time on her hands. It was on their second anniversary when she told Thad, "I think it is time we thought about having a baby."

"No, absolutely not." He was so adamant about it that he shook his finger in her face. Yasmine thought he was going to hit her.

"Why, Thad? We both work, we have a house and good investments, and your mother wants a grandchild."

"You don't have anything but those country bumpkin relatives of yours. I have a house and investments and you probably wouldn't have a job if it wasn't for me."

Yasmine cringed in her seat. Usually his abuse was silence and disregard for her. It was never verbal abuse. His words stunned her.

Thad grabbed her by her throat and held her face to his and said, "If you run and tell my mother, I swear you'll live to regret it."

Then, he smiled at her, got out of the car, and opened the door for her saying, "Watch your step honey."

The next day, Yasmine went through the work day in a daze. She wanted to talk about it, but Thad had threatened her not to talk to his mother. Ava had been against the wedding all along, and Yasmine knew her mother would tell her how fortunate she was to have a man like Thad. The hurt was almost enough to strangle her. Of her choices of confidants, Ava seemed the best.

Ava half-heartedly listened to Yasmine as she watched a Barbara Walters interview. She knew better than to do anything other than listen, especially when it came to Thad. Yasmine said she had considered getting pregnant and not telling Thad until it was too late, but she resolved herself to wait and re-introduce the subject in a couple of months when life smoothed out again.

The months and years went by and Yasmine began to be hopeful. Thad began to be more pleasant. It should have made her happy, but there was something that she couldn't put her finger on.

"Ava, I'm sure he's seeing someone else," Yasmine whined.

"Yasie, it's probably just your imagination."

"I know it's not my imagination. I can tell."

"Well you say he's not out at night and you all work together in the same building. If it was someone at work you'd know about it."

"I'm not crazy. I've been married to this man for almost seven years and he's different."

"Different how?"

"He's happy. This morning he poured me a glass of juice and even laughed out loud at an article in the paper. Then he gave it to me to read. Ava, he's never done that."

"Well, Yasie, isn't that what you wanted? For him to be happy and respond to you as his wife?"

"I want those things, but I know there is another woman. I can't figure out when, where or how, but I know he is seeing someone else."

"Yasie, he's happy and he's treating you nice. Just go with the flow and maybe things will work out."

"Maybe you're right."

The feeling wouldn't leave Yasmine; she was hatching a plan to find out the truth. Charlie looked up as Yasmine, tapped on his door.

"Hey stranger! Where have you been? I meant to thank you again for the cake you baked for my birthday. The card was hilarious."

"You're welcome, Charlie. I'm glad you liked it."

Charlie could tell from her expression that this was not a social call.

"Do you have a minute?"

He really didn't, but he could see whatever Yasmine wanted, was important.

"Sure, sit down."

"Charlie, I really would like to get some more field experience. Do you have anything going on that you think might need a fresh face?"

Charlie thought for a minute. "I could use someone to go to London for a week or two to keep an eye on an operation."

"That would be wonderful," Yasmine exclaimed. "When can I leave?"

"Tomorrow night, if you like."

"That will be great."

Charlie filled her in on the op details and ordered her plane tickets.

Yasmine called Thad and said, "Honey, I just found out that I have to go to London on assignment for the next two weeks. We're going to have to cancel with your parents for this weekend. Will you handle that or should I?"

"I have a call in to my dad about a patient. I'll tell him when he calls me back."

"Good, and can you take me to the airport tomorrow night at nine? I hate to leave my car there for two weeks or more."

"No problem, I'll be able to take you to the airport."

Yasmine was all packed when Thad arrived home from work. He took her bags and instead of dropping her off at curbside as usual, he decided to come in. He gave her a quick peck on the cheek as she got ready to enter the security screening.

The London trip turned out to be a good distraction for Yasmine. The agents she worked with were top of the line and she was a great help to them. They wrapped early. The Mission Chief loved her, so he didn't gripe when she asked if she could stay around a few more days to see the sights.

Yasmine was extremely happy when she finished her work in London and boarded a plane bound for Dallas. Instead of using the Bureau ticket, Yasmine bought another ticket in an alias that she had acquired. She wanted to get home without the Bureau's or Thad's knowledge. When Yasmine stopped by the Budget car rental counter and rented a non-descript sedan, the clerk boldly flirted with her, assuming she really was the slight built man, with a crooked mustache and effeminate hands that she pretended to be.

Yasmine drove to her neighborhood, but pulled into the garage of the empty house across the street. Her neighbors had been transferred and had given her keys to keep an eye on things until the house was sold. She set up surveillance and soon, she saw Thad arrive home, carrying take-out food. He parked his car in the driveway. This surprised Yasmine because they never left cars in the driveway. FBI personnel took great precautions to secure their vehicles. They had a three-car garage, a space for his car, her car, and the 65 mustang that he was refurbishing.

Yasmine wondered aloud, "Why would his car be in the driveway?"

She thought it was very strange, *'Maybe he is about to go out?'* Hours later Thad's car was still parked in the driveway. When night fell silent and the street was clear of neighbors, Yasmine made her way across the street and into her house. She checked the garage. There was a silver Lexus parked where Thad's car should be. Yasmine slipped unnoticed into the house. There were remnants of Popeye's fried chicken in the kitchen, which was not something Thad normally ate. He thought it barbaric to eat meat directly from a bone, saying cavemen did that, not civilized people.

As she made her way up the stairs, she heard Barry White playing on the CD player and she heard voices coming from her bedroom. The bedroom was filled with scented candles. She stood in the door and listened as she heard, Thad say, "Oh my God, you're so good."

In the dark, she heard moaning. She could see her husband making passionate love to someone else.

He was kissing her and touching her, and saying, "You're wonderful. How does it feel? Oh, I've wanted you for so long."

Yasmine stood frozen by the sights and sounds of her husband making love to another woman. He was so loving and passionate. He had never been that way with her. There was a rustling of the sheets as the couple changed positions, now Thad's lover was on top and Thad was moaning.

"Oh, that feels so good, please don't stop. You feel so good."

Yasmine couldn't wait to see who she was. She wanted to scratch the eyes out of the whore who was bold enough to fuck her husband in her bed. Thad grabbed his partner and flipped her back on the bottom and even though Yasmine had never heard that sound from her husband, she knew he was having a massive orgasm. His lover was moaning with delight as Yasmine flipped on the light to see the whore. Yasmine stood frozen; she couldn't believe her eyes.

*****

Yasmine fled the house and drove back to the airport. She had thirty minutes to board an American flight to Atlanta, where Ava was now living. She pulled herself together and bought a ticket. The same clerk was on duty at the Budget Rental counter, and he couldn't believe what he was seeing; the slight man was now a tall woman with a tear-stained face. Yasmine ignored his stares and made her way to the bathroom to fix her disguise.

The knock on the door was urgent, the kind of knock that meant distress. The continuous knocking jarred Ava out of a sound sleep. She looked at the clock. It was almost 3 am and she had only been asleep about an hour. Who would be knocking on her door this time in the morning? Ava sat straight up in her bed and tried to decide whether she was dreaming or not.

She was afraid to answer the door. Ava had no idea who it might be, but she knew there was some urgency. She eased to the door, as the knocking grew more frantic. Through the peephole, Ava saw someone who looked like Yasmine. But the frantic looking woman could not be her friend.

"May I help you?" asked Ava.

"Open the door, Ava, it's me."

Ava opened the door and Yasmine fell into her arms.

"Yasie, what's wrong with you?"

Ava tried to move her out of the doorway, but Yasmine just fell to her knees. Ava pulled her up to the sofa and then ran to get a wet towel.

Returning, she asked, "What happened to you, Yasie?"

Yasmine couldn't answer. Her eyes were swollen, her make-up was smeared, the residue from her fake beard made her face sticky. Ava thought Yasie was having a nervous breakdown. She took her friend in her arms and rocked her as one would rock a colicky baby. Humming softly, Ava rubbed Yasmine's hair as she curled into a fetal position. After about an hour, Yasmine fell asleep. Ava sat with her until the sun came up, she didn't want to move and wake her, so she was relieved when the phone rang at 7:00 am.

Yasmine said, "f that's Thad, please don't let him know I'm here."

It was Thad. "Ava, please forgive me for disturbing you so early in the morning," he said. "but I was wondering, have you heard from Yasmine?"

Ava, fishing for information, said, "Yes, I talked to her in London two days ago. Is everything alright?"

"I'm sure she is fine. I was looking for her. It appears that she left London and I'm wondering about her whereabouts."

"What do you mean you're wondering about her whereabouts? Did something happen that would make you need to wonder?"

Ava could tell that Thad wanted to end the conversation immediately, but she kept firing questions at him. "Do you know for sure that she left London?" she asked.

"I'm sure she left London, she came home briefly and then she left," Thad replied.

"When she was home briefly where did she say she was going?"

"She did not say," Thad said matter-of-factly. "Otherwise, I would know where she is."

"Thad you're not making any sense. Could you start from the beginning?"

"No, Ava, I don't have time. If she contacts you please ask her to call me."

Ava started to say, 'Okay,' but Thad had hung up. She turned to Yasie.

"Do you want to tell me what this is all about?"

"I told you I thought he was cheating on me," Yasmine said.

"I know, you told me. But what happened?"

"I came home early from London and I caught him in the act."

"You caught him with another woman?"

"No, I didn't catch him with another woman."

"Yasie, you're not making any sense. Did you or did you not catch him cheating."

"I did catch him, but not with another woman. He was with Charlie, my boss. Ava he was with a man. And he was really into it, he was kissing him and telling him that he loved him, they had candles lit and Barry White music in the background. Thad was tender and loving. And in seven years he had never been that way with me."

Ava couldn't manage to wipe the shocked look from her face. She sat with her mouth open, looking at her friend. She could not think of anything to say.

"I was fully prepared to confront his woman and pull every strand of hair out of her head, but what do you do if you catch your husband with a man? How do you handle that? What do you say about that? What do you call him? Is a man who fucks your husband a whore? And to make it so bad, he was fucking my boss--the person I trusted and confided in. Charlie, of all people. How do I go on? You told me not to marry him. Go ahead and say 'I told you so!"

"Yasie, I'm sorry. I was right. I'd prayed I was wrong. Believe me I don't want to rub it in your face. It's not that important for me to be right. I want to help you get through this."

After a long pause Yasmine said, "I don't know where to start."

"Honey, you start by deciding what is best for you. Everybody will have an opinion, but this is your life. You decide what is best for you and whatever you decide I'm going to be here to support you and cheer you on."

"Ava, I'm so sorry for all the things I said to you. I was so mad. I didn't want to hear what you were saying. You're the only friend I have and I treated you so mean. All you were trying to do was help me. I was mad because I just loved him so much and I didn't want to hear you tell me that he didn't love me. I didn't want to face that reality. I wanted to believe that deep down, he really loved me. I wanted to live in my own little fantasy world where Thad adored me. I really thought we were going to live happily ever after. I'm sorry for the names I called you and everything else I said."

"All is forgiven. I know you didn't mean any of it."

Yasmine squeezed Ava's hand and said, "Thank you for everything. Thank you for still being my friend, even though I was such a bitch to you. I can't believe that you even opened the door for me. That's why I didn't call first."

"You're like my sister, I'll always open the door for you."

"Don't you have to go to work today?"

"No. I took off. My boyfriend, Ronnie, and I were going to go away for a long weekend, but there was a break-in at his store so he is stuck doing inventory, so I'm free as a bird."

Yasmine and Ava talked all day. Yasmine felt a sense of comfort that she hadn't felt for many years. After four days away, Yasmine packed up and went home to her beautiful house and her beautiful husband.

1 .   Yasmine should realize

    A.   The part she played in the situation.

    B.   Every marriage has problems.

    C.   She was deceived.

2 .   Yasmine should

    A.   Get a divorce.

    B.   Go back to her husband.

    C.   Call Thad out and let the world know.

3 .   Yasmine should

    A.   Respect Thad's privacy.

    B.   Use Thad's secret to make him do what she wants.

    C.   Use Thad's secret to blackmail Thad and Charlie.

4 .   Yasmine should

    A.   Quit her job.

    B.   Go to work and act as if nothing had happened.

    C.   Start a scandal at work.

5 .   Yasmine should

    A.   Help Thad keep his secret from his parents.

    B.   Act as if nothing has happened.

    C.   Tell Thad's parents what she knows.

6 .   Yasmine should

    A.   Leave the house.

    B.   Insist that the house be sold and split the profits.

    C.   Take the house.

7 .   Yasmine should

    A.   Get personal therapy.

    B.   Get couples therapy with Thad.

    C.   Insist that Thad goes to therapy.

8 .   Yasmine should

    A.   Leave the marriage with nothing.

    B.   Stay in the marriage.

    C.   Try to clean Thad out in the divorce.

9 .   Yasmine

    A.   Should apologize to Thad.

    B.   Make Thad apologize to her.

    C.   Get revenge instead of an apology.

1 0 .   Yasmine should

    A.   Try to maintain a friendship with Thad.

    B.   Maintain the status quo.

    C.   Let Thad and Charlie feel her rage.

1 1 .   Yasmine should

    A.   Feel no fear.

    B.   Feel secure.

    C.   Be afraid.

If your answers total

        Mostly A's read ending X

        Mostly B's read ending Y

        Mostly C's read ending Z

Ending X

Yasmine's FBI experience really came in handy. By the time her plane landed, she had arranged for movers to store her things and had rented a small corporate apartment. Four days with Ronnie and Ava showed her what she was missing. She'd trade all the possessions she had to feel the love Ava had.

She was not surprised to see Thad waiting for her when she stepped onto the curb to hail a cab. She started to ignore him, but decided not to put off the inevitable.

"I was worried sick about you," he said.

"Is that so?"

"Yes, it is so. I know you had to be upset."

"Thad, let's cut to the chase. I owe you an apology."

"No, No.   . . ."

"I pushed myself into your life, when you told me time after time in word and deed that you didn't want me. But I saw what I wanted and I totally disregarded your feelings."

"Yasmine . . . "

"I'm not finished! Now I understand why you didn't want me. Or maybe you wouldn't have wanted me if you weren't gay."

"I'm not Gay!!! Yasmine, I'm not gay."

"What do you call a man who sleeps with a man?"

"I'm not gay. I'm primarily a top."

"Top, bottom, middle, sideways, it's all the same to me. But that has nothing to do with it. You didn't want me and I thought I loved you enough for both of us. Now, I see that it really does take two."

"But, I do love you in my own way."

"Well, Thad, your way is not working for me. I want to be in a relationship where my husband desires me, wants to know what I think, reaches out for me at night, and wants to make love to me."

"We can work on it."

"No, Thad, I've made your life miserable for long enough. I want a quiet divorce, I don't want anything, I want my name back, and I'll forever keep your secret."

"Yasie, it doesn't have to end this way. We can work this out. We can get counseling and maybe think about having a couple of kids."

"No, Thad, I'm ready to start over."

"What if I won't give you a divorce?"

"Well that's up to you, Thad. But I want to give you your life back."

"But, my parents are going to want to know why."

"Tell them whatever you want, and I'll agree with you. Tell them I'm to blame. I cheated on you, whatever you want. I don't care."

"But, they love you."

"I know, Thad, but you can't live a lie your whole life, trying to please your parents."

"So, you just want to walk out on all we have?"

"Thad, I realized that all we have are material things, but now I know that's not enough for me. I thought it was what I wanted, but it's not enough ... I saw Ronnie come up behind Ava in the kitchen, when she was cooking. He hugged her from behind, and then he kissed her for no reason. I could feel the passion between them. It was in that moment that I knew I'd trade everything for that," Yasmine said, with a faraway look in her eyes.

"So you want me to kiss you in the kitchen?"

"No, Thad! I want you to find someone you want to kiss in the kitchen. I don't want to be the woman who will resort to anything to get or keep a man. I did that with you and all it got me was heartache. I'm sorry I forced myself on you, Thad."

"But Yasie, we had some good times ..."

"The movers will be here tomorrow at 10:00 am. I've rented a corporate apartment and I'm going to finish up a few cases, then ask Charlie to transfer me to London. Under the circumstances, I think he'll be agreeable. I enjoyed my work there and I think London will be the perfect distraction."

"Will you give me a chance to make it up to you? I can be the man you want. I know I can."

"Thad, you are who you are."

They rode the rest of the way home in silence. Yasmine felt a little nostalgic when Thad turned onto their street and raised the garage door to their beautiful home that she had spent years decorating. Yasmine walked through the house, touching and seeing things as if she were seeing them for the first time.

She walked from room to room, as if she were saying goodbye to good friends. She fought back the tears as she opened the door to the guest room, where she would spend her last night.

The move went like clockwork. Yasmine put blue dots on everything going to storage and orange dots on everything going to the apartment. Within twenty-four hours Yasmine was standing on the balcony of her little apartment. Her divorce attorney didn't understand why she didn't want to take Thad to the cleaners. Thad said he would not consider signing the papers unless she took at least half a million dollars as set up money in the pre-nup. She agreed, and used it to set up a scholarship fund in Thad's mother's name.

After three years of therapy, Yasmine began to feel confident again. She got in touch with her feelings and her need for attention. Growing up with so many siblings, she hadn't received the attention that she needed and felt she would disappear if she couldn't find a way to be the center of attention. In London, she got the attention she needed and was promoted three times in two years. After almost three years, Yasmine was ready to return to the states.

Yasmine's plane arrived a little early in Atlanta. She spotted Ava on the ascending escalators as she was going down. Once they were united, the two women hugged a long time.

"So, how are you, Miss Mommy?" Yasmine asked.

"Sleep deprived, fat and happy."

"Oh, you're not that FAT," Yasmine said, looking over her Gucci sunglasses.

"Bitch."

"Fat Bitch."

The two laughed and waited for Yasmine's luggage to show up. Ronnie was waiting in the car with the baby.

"Give me my God son, I demand him now," Yasmine said in her best British accent.

"Don't I at least get a hi, hello, or something?"

"Yes, you do" Yasmine said, pecking Ronnie on his check

"He is beautiful, the most beautiful baby I've ever seen." Yasmine snuggled up to little Tyler. The admiration seemed mutual, they both cooed and smiled.

Ava was frantic, there were fifty people coming from around the world for the baby's christening and the reception afterward. Yasmine took over the details and sent Ava to take a nap, while Ronnie made another airport run. The caterers were setting up and Yasmine was arranging flowers, between stealing kisses from little Tyler. She wiped her hands on a towel, when the doorbell rang. The man at the door, cleared his throat,

"Oh, ma'am, I'm sorry. I must be at the wrong house. I'm looking for Ava and Ronnie."

"Come in, I'm Yasmine. Ava is taking a much needed nap and Ronnie is on his way to the airport."

"Oh, I'm Jackson, Ronnie's cousin and godfather extraordinaire."

"Well, you better be, because I'm godmother and I will be watching your every move."

Jackson laughed and soon fell right in, helping to cross things off the To-do list to make the backyard tent into a beautiful dining hall. Jackson switched the place cards so he would be seated next to Yasmine. He wasn't strikingly handsome like Thad, but he had a quiet charm that sent Yasmine to check her clothes and make-up.

The affair was a great success. When all the guests were gone and Tyler was settled in, Yasmine and Jackson sent Ronnie and Ava to bed while they cleaned up and put all the food away. Jackson pulled out his CD player and put on some music to make the tasks go faster. A couple of times they stopped their work to dance. It was the most fun Yasmine had had in years. They stayed up all night talking. The three days they spent together were magical. They took Tyler everywhere they went and blushed when people said he looked just like one or the other.

Ava was a little jealous because she didn't get to see much of her friend. She stormed into her room at 6:00 am on Yasmine's final day in town.

"So, tell all! You and Jackson have been spending an awful lot of time together. What's the deal?"

"Well, we have been going over the god-parents handbook. Making sure we adhere to all the principles, procedures, policies, and responsibilities of the job."

"Yasie, it's me you're talking to."

"Yeah, I know. He's wonderful, attractive, intelligent and did I mention, oh, so sexy!" They both laughed.

"He sure is sexy, but don't ever tell Ronnie I said that."

"Girl, there is something about him that makes me want to get naked, plus I enjoy his company. I'm just a little leery."

"I can understand that, but he's a lot different from Thad. He is kind and considerate and I think you two would be good for each other."

"Maybe."

"You know, I'd love to have you in Atlanta. You could get a transfer from London so you could spend some time with Tyler and hopefully, give him a little cousin to play with."

"Well, that's not a bad idea, but we'll have to see what Jackson says about it."

"Well, according to what I've heard . . ." Ava said, walking toward the door glancing over her shoulder.

"What did he say? Come on tell me."

Yasmine caught Ava before she got out the door and snatched her back into the room.

"Okay, Nosey," Ava laughed. "Jackson told Ronnie, that he has never met anyone like you. He thinks you could be the one. But he doesn't want to move too fast and scare you off."

"We'll see, but I think I agree with him."

Ending Y

Thad was waiting for Yasmine when she exited the jet way. He took her carryon bag for her and they headed for home. The ride was completely quiet. When they arrived home Thad took her bag upstairs and ordered Thai food for dinner. Yasmine took a bath and watched TV until the food was delivered. They ate in silence and Yasmine cleared the table and decided to answer her e-mails, while Thad took a shower and got ready for bed.

"I want to have a baby," Yasmine said while Thad was brushing his teeth.

"Okay."

"I want a new house and a new bed."

"Okay."

"I'm quitting work, once the baby comes."

"Okay."

"And, I want you to break it off with Charlie."

Turning to look at her, with a pleading look in his eyes, Thad said, "Okay."

Yasmine was ecstatic that she conceived so quickly. The pregnancy was textbook and Thad's parents were anxiously awaiting their grandchild. Thad was even happy to see his parents so happy. Little Thad was a beautiful baby with grand toothless grins that reduced adults to mindless baby talk and joy.

Little Thad was a gifted child, he played sports with his dad, spoke French and Italian with his mom, learned classical piano for Thad's parents and learned to play cards and dominoes for Yasmine's family. Yasmine and Thad's life totally revolved around their son. He was the source of love and pride in a loveless house. People on the outside thought they had everything. They each played their roles, their pictures were plastered all over the society pages for their generosity to the community, but if you looked behind their eyes, the sadness wasn't too hard to find.

Ending Z

Yasmine walked into the Bureau Director's office. She had waited almost two weeks for the appointment. She was shocked to see Charlie sitting in the office. She wanted this to be a surprise attack, but somehow the word was out. She thought she'd been hiding her moves carefully, but Charlie and Thad seemed to be one step ahead of her.

"Director Sinclair, thank you so much for seeing me."

"My pleasure, now what can I do for you?" the Director said, waving her to the chair next to Charlie's."

"Sir, with all due respect, I had hoped to have a conversation with you alone."

"Agent Morgan, I'm not in the habit of having conversations with agents, that's why I have field supervisors, managers, and deputy directors."

"Sir, my issue is with my manager and I didn't think it was appropriate to discuss this particular problem with him."

"Yasmine, you don't want to do this. I'm sure we can work this out," Charlie said, grabbing her hand.

"No we can't, Charlie!" Yasmine pulled her hand back.

"What do you want to do, share my husband?"

"Yasmine, don't do this." Charlie rose to try and calm her down. "You shouldn't have done this!" Charlie said

"You shouldn't be fucking my husband. Get your hands off me, you fucking faggot."

Yasmine stormed out of the director's office and headed for the elevator. Charlie closed the door behind her.

Yasmine knew she was in trouble; the FBI had many ways to bring people to their knees. She carefully outlined her plan to extract the revenge she felt she deserved. She knew she was playing a dangerous game; she had too many insider secrets stored in her head for them to leave her alone. She wrote seven letters, which contained the most important secrets --in case of her untimely demise.

*****

The car that jumped the curb while Yasmine was jogging mangled her body. The little 82-year-old lady who had been driving had lost control, causing a horrible accident that got top billing on the news. Yasmine was buried with a simple graveside ceremony. Thad did an excellent job acting as the grieving widower. Yasmine's family was well taken care of with the million dollars in insurance money and they were pleased that Thad and his family gave scholarships in her name to her high school and college and built a park in her honor.

Yasmine's letters to the press were intercepted, making Charlie smile over the neat job he and Thad had done. The only person who suspected the truth was Ava, who knew she was being watched and monitored, so she kept quiet for fear of her

own safety. Ronnie convinced Ava that she could not fight the
FBI and win.

Marva

Max smiled as he looked through the scope of his assault rifle. There was something about a fresh kill that excited him. His big beefy fingers hovered above the trigger as he looked for a clean shot. He was about to squeeze the trigger when his cell phone rang and broke his concentration.

"Yeah!"

"Max, did you do the job?"

"No, I'm in position now."

"The Boss said, abort."

"Abort? I've been following this guy for three days, trying to get a clean hit."

"The Boss called it off. You'll still get your $50,000, but the Boss has changed his mind."

"Fine with me. It's his money."

"Check the place. The other half of your money will be there in an hour."

*****

"Trisha, where are you? I've been waiting for fifteen minutes!" Marva said in her most irritated tone.

"Girl, I had to stop by the salon and get a nail fixed. I can't go clubbing with chipped polish. They'd take away DIVA points for that. I'll be there in a few minutes. Just sit tight."

"And why didn't you call to let me know! You're wasting my time. I've got better things to do than sit around the parking lot of a nightclub. And where is Monica? Is she coming?"

"Marva, don't get your drawers in a knot! I'm sure she's on her way, so please don't start your negative routine. We're going to have fun tonight. Go in and score us a table before it gets too crowded. You know how happy hour gets."

Trisha knew all the happening places where the up and coming liked to hang out. She flipped her cell phone, shook her head, and said, "That girl is much too high strung."

Marva got out of her new red two-seater Mercedes and walked to the entrance of Minion's, the new hot spot in town. She clicked the security button and watched the lights flicker. She smiled, admiring her new car. As Marva approached the door, a well dressed man, wearing a custom fit suit and black Kenneth Cole shoes, held the door for her. Her words said, 'Thank you' but her mind said, *Where have you been all my life? Are you married? Do you like women?* In her mind, she asked a myriad of other questions that women with biological clocks ticking ask when they see a good-looking man, who is obviously successful and in the right age bracket. Thankfully, he responded to her spoken words.

"You're welcome. The pleasure is all mine."

He was not necessarily a good-looking man, but he had a look about him that said, *I'm sure of myself, I'm in control, I'm the man that can tame your roar.* His body was long and thick: a boxer's body and his obviously expensive suit made him look even better. He approached two other men standing by the bar and performed the 'secret handshake' that guys have, the one with a shoulder bump on the end. She wondered where men went to learn all the different handshakes. Was there a handshake handbook?

Marva surveyed the club, taking in the opulence of it. The club looked more like a lavish resort than a local nightclub. There were stunning chandeliers, expensive wall coverings and the furniture looked as if it would have fit nicely in someone's multi-million dollar home. The mahogany bar shone like glass. All the wait-staff were dressed in black priest collar shirts and black pants, with matching rhinestone belts. The crowd was sparse, but building. Marva chose a high top table near the bar, close to two of the four large dance floors. She felt awkward sitting there alone, so she surveyed the place, being careful not to make eye contact with anyone.

"May I get you something from the bar," came a voice from her left. Marva reveled at the sight of the muscle bound waiter.

"Yes, I'll have a Brandy Alexander," Marva said with a flirt in her voice.

"Right away."

The waiter scurried away and returned in what seemed like seconds with drink in hand.

"How much do I owe, you?"

"Nothing ma'am. Your drink has been paid for."

"And who do I need to thank for that?" asked Marva, her flirt growing bolder.

The waiter stopped and pointed to the gentleman who had opened the door for her.

She smiled and mouthed, "Thank you."

He nodded and returned to his friends.

Marva sat and shifted back and forth, uncomfortable at being alone in a bar.

Just as she made up her mind to leave, her friend Monica tapped her on her shoulder.

"Hey Ms. Thang, sorry I'm late. I got stopped by one of my students who was trying to convince me to let him pass, even though he's missed more than 60% of the classes and two papers."

"Well, what did you tell him?"

Monica put her purse of the table. "I told him   I'm sure you will pass my class, when you take it again next semester."

Marva laughed and Monica settled into a seat next to her.

"What's that you're drinking?"

Marva let Monica sample her drink and Monica waved for the waiter. In an instant the muscle bound man was back. The waiter came and took Monica's drink order. The two women commented on the lavishness of the club and all the young handsome men who were there.

"And where is Trisha?" asked Monica.

"Oh, you know Trisha. She was getting her nails done, getting ready to make her 'grand entrance.'" The two laughed and relaxed to the music that the D. J. was playing.

They chatted easily, catching up on the details of their lives and work.

Trisha arrived an hour later.

"Well, hello ladies."

"Hey girl! What took you so long?" exclaimed Marva and Monica, in unison.

Trisha ignored the comment and walked to the bar--eyeing the well dressed gentlemen there. Trisha made a point of leaning over so more of her cleavage would show. She looked good in her hot pink spandex mini-dress. The little number exposed one shoulder, showing off the tattoo of her name in Egyptians symbols. The dress also revealed one hip on the opposite side of the missing shoulder. It was probably a size four, even though it wouldn't have hurt her to get a six. Her sandals strapped midway up her calf, showing off her shapely legs. The sandals were the same shade of pink as her nail polish, blush and eye shadow.

"Look at her, scouting her prey. I bet she had to grease herself to get in that dress," laughed Monica.

"No, they spray painted it on, but if I had a body like hers."

Monica interrupted, "But you do have a body like hers. You just chose to dress like a respectable woman your age. And for about $5,000, you can have those breasts, and for another $5,000 the flat stomach."

They both laughed. Trisha came back to the table, glancing over her shoulder to see who was watching.

"Trisha, you never did say what took you so long," said Marva.

"Well, I went in to get my nail fixed and Stella told me about this place that will tattoo your eyeliner, lip liner or eyebrow arches on, so I had to check it out."

Trisha leaned over to show her friends her new discovery.

"What do you think? This way you look good all the time, even when you first wake up in the morning."

"Girl, that looks painful," Monica said.

"Only for a few seconds, but it was worth it. I don't have to worry about applying eyeliner again for several months. I'm thinking about getting the eyebrow arch as well, but I didn't have enough time today."

"Did they tattoo that dress on, too?" Marva asked

Trisha smiled. "Jealously won't get you anywhere. Besides, if you got it, flaunt it. And I got it and the men want it."

"Girl, you're going to keep on till you find Mr. Goodbar," Monica commented.

"I'm not looking for Mr. Goodbar. I want Mr. Good Dick or Mr. Good Money. It would be great if they are the same man, but I'll take either," smirked Trisha.

The girls laughed. They'd been friends since third grade. They made it a point to get together at least once a month, and they talked almost every day.

"Marva, how are things at good ole' National Airlines?" asked Trisha. "I hear you are about to lay off some people."

"Well, that's true. But, mostly reservation and customer service people. I don't think I'll be affected."

"Management is never affected. You get raises while everybody else is scrambling to find new jobs." Trisha saw the frown taking over Marva's face, and turned her attention to Monica.

"How are things in higher learning?"

"Good. I'm doing my part in the quest to shape young minds. You know the life of a college professor is not nearly as glam as that of a hairdresser or airline exec. By the way, which one of your rich clients told you about this place?"

"Bobbi told me about it. She works for a record company and is always in the know about where the talent hangs out."

"Well, this place is jumping," Marva said.

As the club filled, the music seemed to get better and better. Several men approached the table and asked to dance with Trisha, but she'd size them up and turn them down for one reason or another: cheap shoes, raggedy finger nails, old suit, too much cologne or--the worst-- fake jewelry.

When Darren, the gentlemen who'd held the door for Marva and purchased her drink, approached the table, Trisha murmured under her breath, "Damn, could this be my lucky day? Now that's what I'm talking about."

He greeted all three women, but turned his attention to Marva.

"Would you like to dance with me?"

"She doesn't dance, but I certainly do," Trisha said.

Darren didn't acknowledge Trisha; he kept looking at Marva.

"Of course, I would love to," said Marva, rolling her eyes at Trisha.

Darren took Marva's elbow, helped her from the tall chair, and led her to the dance floor, where they danced to 'Brown Sugar,' by D'Angelo. After the song was over, the two linked arms and he led her back to her table. He thanked her and nodded at the other women as he was leaving.

Marva stopped him and said, "By the way, my name is Marva Danzy."

Darren introduced himself and presented his hand for a handshake. There was no sophisticated shake or shoulder bump at the end. She thought the shoulder bump must be reserved for men.

"It's very nice to meet you, even though we unofficially met at the door earlier," Darren said.

He thanked her again and excused himself, returning to the bar with his friends. He sent the waiter to the table with a red rose and another Brandy Alexander for Marva.

She smiled at Darren and mouthed the words "Thank you" in his direction. Darren tipped his glass to her and returned to the conversation with the other men.

"He looks a little cock-eyed to me," Trisha said.

"Well, he looks damned good to me," Monica said

"Me too, Monica," Marva said. "Besides, you're just jealous that the early bird got to dance with the good looking man."

"Let's just hope the early bird doesn't get worms!" Trisha said.

Monica and Marva laughed.

Trisha swung her long curly weave around as she scanned the room to see who was worthy of her time. The women laughed and popped their fingers to the music and talked about old and new business. They danced when their 'songs' came on and watched others dance. Darren and Marva made eye contact several times during the night. He stayed close to the bar, talking to the other well dressed men. Trisha identified one of them as a member of the city council and another as a local high profile attorney.

As Darren was leaving, he came to the table.

"Ms. Danzy, I just wanted to say again how good it was to meet you. I have an early day in the morning so I'm going to have to leave. I hope our paths will cross again. Oh, by the way, I left an open tab and the waiter will get you and your friends whatever you want."

As his friends approached, he excused himself and left. Marva was a little disappointed since he didn't even ask for her phone number.

"Don't be too disappointed. That cock-eyed fool was probably gay," said Trisha.

*****

An early morning phone call from Trisha interrupted the visions of sugarplums-- and Darren--dancing in Marva's head. Marva looked at the clock; it was 6:17 am. She picked up the phone.

"Trisha, somebody better be dead if you're calling me this early on a Saturday morning."

"No, girl. Ain't nobody dead, I just need a favor. I need to borrow $500. Until the end of the month."

"Trish, I can't lend you any more money. You haven't paid me back the last three times I lent you money. You already owe me $1400."

"Oh, girl, come on! What's $1400 among friends? You know you're my girl and you know I'm good for it."

"Fourteen hundred dollars may not seem like much to you, especially when it's my money, but I have to draw the line somewhere. Trisha, you're going to have to learn to live within your means."

"I don't need a sermon. I need $500. Two of my stylists didn't pay their booth rent, so I'm short. I promise I'll pay you the whole $1,900, back at the end of the month.

"Okay, but you're going to have to sign an IOU and give me a postdated check."

"I can't believe you're acting like that after all the years we've been friends!"

"That's the thing. I'm your friend not your financer."

"Okay, I'll sign the damn IOU and give you the damn check, but I'm beginning to feel like we don't have a real friendship. You know I'd do it for you if the tables were turned."

"The guilt trip won't work. Besides, I've always been there for you and being there for you always costs me."

"Fine, then if that's the way you want it. Can I come by in an hour to get my money?"

"I don't have that kind of cash on me."

"I'll take a check if you have some ID."

"You're a fool. You know that don't you?" Marva said laughing at her friend.

Trisha said, "No you're the fool! I'll be over around eight."

Later, Marva stumbled to the door in her bathrobe and gave Trisha the check.

"Thanks girl, you know I needed it. Oh, by the way, who was that guy you were talking to at the club last night?"

Marva smiled, remembering the sight and smell of Darren.

"His name is Darren and that's about all there is to tell."

"He looked cock-eyed to me."

"Get out of here, Trisha! I've got things to do."

Marva was strolling through the Whole Foods Market examining the organic fresh fruits and vegetables, when someone tapped her on the shoulder. Marva turned to discover Darren smiling down at her. She thought, *Something told me to dress better* as she glanced down at her faded jeans and sweatshirt.

"Fancy meeting you here. I must be living right."

"Darren, what a surprise."

"That's a good sign. You remembered my name."

"Of course, I remember. I don't think I could forget if I tried."

Marva realized she was flirting and it felt good. She hadn't been interested in a man since Lloyd left six years ago.

"I come here every Saturday but, I've never seen you here. I know, because if I had, I would have stopped to notice and admire," Darren told her.

Marva blushed and Darren took her little red mini grocery basket from her hand as he steered her out of the path of a little girl pushing a basket right toward them. Marva was so taken by Darren that she couldn't remember what she had come to the store for. They walked and talked through the store as if they had known each other from way back in the day.

After the shopping was done, Darren took Marva's hand. "Miss Danzy, if you're not too busy, why don't you have lunch with me? I know a great little vegetarian restaurant not far away."

"Veggie Tables?"

"You know it?"

"I go there all the time.

"So do I. I can't believe we've been crossing each other's paths and haven't met before."

Lunch was easy. They talked and joked with each other and enjoyed their meals. Marva was totally relaxed with him. Talking to him was just like talking to one of the girls.

After an hour and a half, Darren said, "Marva, I'm so glad I got to see you again. You're quite an incredible woman. I've enjoyed talking to you, but I have a business meeting scheduled so I have to get going."

Marva was sad to see lunch end. Darren walked her to her car and gave her hand a gentle squeeze before he waved goodbye and walked to his midnight blue BMW. Marva couldn't believe he didn't ask for her phone number. *He must be married*, she thought. But he wasn't wearing a ring and he didn't mention anything about a family. However, a man as good looking and successful as he was must have a wife or girlfriend somewhere.

Marva decided to let the top down on her convertible and let the wind soothe her soul. She put her favorite Rachelle Ferrell CD on and headed for the freeway. She thought, *At least I had lunch with a handsome man who is polite and gentlemanly. That has to count for something.* Marva decided to stop by the nursery to get plants for her front yard. She always worked in the yard when she had something to think about. There was nothing more calming than having dirt under her nails.

By the end of the week, Marva was exhausted. It had been a busy week and she was glad to see Friday come. As she was leaving for the day, her cell phone rang. Marva recognized Monica's voice.

"Hey Ms. Thang, what's up for the weekend?"

"I don't know, girl. I'm so tired I think I'm going to stay home and just catch up on some reading. My mother sent me this great new book from Oprah's book club.

"If you want to do some reading I have plenty of bad term papers. Maybe several of them would help you."

Marva laughed. "NO, girl! Don't do me any favors. Please, not the bad term papers!"

"I know. I really don't want to read them myself. Well, I was calling to see if you wanted to go out tonight."

"I'm not in the mood for a club. Maybe a light dinner or something?"

Later, Monica was waiting outside the little neighborhood Bistro when Marva drove up.

"Change of plans," she told Marva. "The place is closed for a private party."

After some discussion, they decided to go downtown to a little jazz club that also had a grille.

"Well, when was the last time you talked to Darren?"

"There have been no Darren sightings. He must be married or not interested. He didn't ask for my phone number or anything and I don't have his."

"Maybe he's just shy," Monica said.

"Did you see him? He's not shy. Maybe he's gay."

"Well, I watched the two of you dancing and he doesn't move like a gay man. He never took his eyes off your butt. And speaking of dancing, where did you learn those moves?" Monica asked.

Marva said, "Soul Trainnnnn."

With the evening winding down, Marva said, "Thanks for inviting me out. Dinner was good and the music was soothing. Just what the doctor ordered."

"Anything to postpone reading term papers."

The next day, Marva woke early and dressed in her cute workout clothes—the ones, that were never supposed to see sweat. When she arrived at the Whole Foods Market, she drove around the parking lot looking for Darren's car. She hoped she'd run into him. Marva said half aloud and half to herself, "Well, he hasn't shown up and I've been here almost two hours. I better get out of here before security starts to think I'm stalking the lettuce."

On the drive home, Marva gave herself a good talking to. 'What is wrong with you? You're acting like a teenager with your first crush. Pull yourself together. You have plenty to be grateful for. You have a good job, nice car, great friends, beautiful home, you've traveled the world and you have a 401K and good health insurance . . . No matter how much Marva talked to herself, she kept thinking, You're forty-one and you're alone and you're alone and you're alone.

Wednesday evening, Marva was running late for her Pilate's class. As she entered the building and scanned her membership card, she noticed a tall, broad-shouldered man working out in the weight area. It looked like Darren, but she knew she was just imagining things. Marva hurried to her class, which lasted an hour and was on her way out, while chatting with a classmate, when suddenly, Darren tapped her on the shoulder and said, "I thought it was you."

Marva surveyed her clothes. Why do I always run into him when I'm looking like a bum?

However, she managed a polite smile as her classmate waited to be introduced. Darren said hello to her friend, but never took his eyes off of Marva.

"Marva, I can't believe we attend the same gym, shop at the same grocery store and like the same clubs. This must be fate. We've run into each other three times. Don't they say the third time is the charm?" He smiled down at her. "I know I'm charmed."

He took a minute to let Marva complete her blush cycle.

"Do you have plans now? Maybe we can catch our place before it closes."

"Darren, I don't want to go out looking like this. They will think you picked up a homeless person."

"They'll think I'm a lucky man. Besides you look beautiful and natural and I love your hair pulled back like that."

This time the blush cycle was long and deep.

"Okay, let me go and freshen up a bit."

Darren was waiting by the door when she returned, and they headed off to Veggie Tables.

Once inside the restaurant, they began talking so much that the waiter had to come to the table three times before they were ready to order. Before they knew it, two hours had flown by and the restaurant was empty and cleaned with all the chairs on the table except theirs.

Looking at her watch, Marva said, "Well, I guess it's time we leave."

Darren got up and helped her with her chair. They decided to go have frozen yogurt cups. Marva started to pay the tab, but Darren interrupted, saying, "You don't ever pull out your wallet with me. I'm a very old fashioned man and if I can't afford to take you out, I'll let you know. I believe in treating my woman well and giving her the world."

The look he gave her made Marva want to jump down on her knees and thank God, Buddha, Allah, and everybody else who had brought this man her way. They talked about everything: work, politics, religion, and even their mothers' maiden names.

Thursday morning, Marva arrived at the office to find a large arrangement of exotic flowers at the security station. As she admired them, Earl, the security guard said, "Ms. Danzy, I was just about to bring them up to your office."

"These are for me?"

"Yes ma'am. I'll bring them up shortly. They are a bit heavy and I wouldn't want you to mess up that pretty dress."

Marva waited the fifteen minutes it took the guard to arrive, and eagerly read the card. It said, 'Here's to the charm.' Marva immediately got on the phone with Monica.

"Take your time and enjoy this. Don't start planning the wedding and for life ever after, you know how we get. Enjoy it for what it's worth."

Marva was on cloud nine for the rest of the day. Everyone admired her flowers and everyone wanted to know what the occasion was and who thought she was special enough to spend that kind of money.

Marva emptied her purse on her desk, thinking that she had lost Darren's business card, which he'd given her at dinner.

It took her a few minutes to find it tucked between the carbon copies of her checkbook. When she called him to thank him for the flowers, Darren invited her to his place for dinner on Friday night.

Marva arrived Friday night wearing a royal blue silk pantsuit. The top was off the shoulder and her toned stomach showed underneath the cropped top. Darren kissed her hand, after turning her around to admire her.

"Wow, I'm a really lucky man."

Marva admired his home, which was in a gorgeous upscale neighborhood on the lake. It was one of those places where ducks walk in the street and each house probably came equipped with a boat and a Mercedes. The place where only beautiful people are allowed to dwell.

"I hope you're hungry."

"Yes, I am. And something smells wonderful."

Darren flipped the oven light on and looked at his creation.

"About five more minutes. While we are waiting, why don't I give you a tour?"

He non-chalantly walked Marva around the five thousand square foot house, it was one of the smallest in the neighborhood.

Marva thought the house didn't seem to have a totally masculine feel. Almost reading her mind, he said, "Some of the things here are not totally my taste. The designer chose the drapes and fabric."

"Well, she did a beautiful job."

The master bathroom looked larger than the entire first floor. The bed had beautiful sheer fabric draped from the four posts, and it sat on a platform about six inches off the floor. A walk down two steps took her to the sitting room, which overlooked the lake. There was a breathtaking balcony decorated with a variety of exotic plants and hanging foliage.

The oven bell rang, and Darren looked at Marva.

"My dear, I do believe dinner is served."

He helped her down the winding staircase to the kitchen, uncorked a bottle of wine, and took Marva out to the deck, where she saw two beautiful place settings with candles and fresh flowers. He pulled the chair out for her and placed the starched linen napkin in her lap. He brought out each course and served her. The main course was grilled shrimp with marinated eggplant and squash with a dill sauce. The conversation was light and free. Marva bragged on his cooking and he seemed to relish the praise. He cleared the table and returned to the deck. They watched the stars and talked, and when Marva looked at her watch, it was almost midnight.

"Well, I guess I'd better go, I have a busy day tomorrow."

She thought he would resist her leaving, but he got up and helped her to her feet from the lounger where she was relaxing. He pulled her close to him and lifted her chin to him. Marva thought, *Finally, he's going to kiss me.*

Instead, Darren looked into her eyes and said, "Marva, I'd like to ask you a question."

Feeling a little woozy from the wine, Marva said, "Sure, Darren, anything."

"I'd like permission to court you, the old fashioned way. I'm interested in getting to know you and finding out all the intriguing facts about your life and your dreams."

"Permission granted, I haven't been courted in a while."

Darren smiled and revealed little dimples at the creases of his mouth. He looked happy as he walked her out. He then pulled a small Tiffany's box out of his pocket and gave it to her, asking her to open it when she got home. Marva couldn't wait 'til she got home; she pulled over at a gas station and opened the box to find a small gold charm made in the shape of a heart. The engraving read, *The third time is the charm.*

Darren was attentive and supportive. He seemed to anticipate her every need. The courtship was marvelous; Marva was the envy of her friends, especially Trisha. Trisha called for her weekly update on all the romantic happenings.

"Hey girl, I'm surprised to catch you home. No one can seem to keep up with you these days," Trisha said.

"I'm sorry girl, Darren has been keeping me busy."

Trisha wanted to know every detail. "Well tell me more about this hot torrid romance of yours."

"Well let's see, last week we went to the Renaissance for dinner. We had to wait several weeks for dinner reservations, and I saw the mayor and his wife there. Then, on Saturday, Darren rented a sailboat and we went out to the Marina and had a picnic on the water. On Sunday, we went to visit one of his friends who is a lawyer and sports agent for some of the top professional athletes. On Monday, he gave me a beautiful bracelet to put my charms on. On Tuesday, we worked out together and went out to eat afterwards. On Wednesday, he surprised me by coming to my office to take me to lunch. On Thursday, we worked out together again and I cooked dinner…my lasagna made with plantains. Friday, we went back to Mignon's. Today he is playing golf and, later we are going to the Mystery Theatre. Tomorrow we are taking a car trip to see an art exhibit."

"It seems like this guy is too good to be true. Don't you feel crowded? It seems you hardly have a minute to yourself. I don't think I could take that smothering."

"That's good, because you don't have to take any of it, I like having my man close."

"Well, that seems a little too close for me. You haven't told me how is he at laying pipe. The old Horizon hoochie-coochie," Trisha said.

"We haven't had sex. Darren says he doesn't want his relationship with me clouded by sex, he wants to have a relationship based on mutual respect and honesty."

"Darren said this. Darren said that. Well, I say "bullshit. You've been going out with this man for nearly two months straight and he's talking about no sex. That cock-eyed fool is crazy, gay or has a really small penis."

"Trisha, you can say what the hell you want. All your dates are banging your head against the headboard before the clock strikes twelve and they are gone before you can roll over and finish a cigarette, so don't say a damn thing to me about someone who cares enough about me to establish a relationship. I'm sorry that I'm not interested in your assembly line."

Trisha was hurt, but in her heart she knew some of what Marva said was true. "Just because I refuse to let cobwebs grow on my ass does not mean that I don't have meaningful relationships. Mark my words, he is either crazy, gay or needle-dick," Trisha, retorted.

"I'm sorry, Trisha. I don't have time to play slum ball with you, I have to get ready for my date with a man who doesn't mind seeing me in the daytime."

Marva hung up the phone and started her bath water. She took a long bath to cool off, thinking, *How dare Trisha? She's just mad that Darren chose me. She just can't handle it!* The rest of the day, Marva caught up on household chores and started to get ready for her date. When Darren arrived, he was very sullen.

"What's wrong, honey?"

"I've got some major decisions to make in the next couple of days and I'm not sure what to do."

Marva patted the space on the sofa next to her.

"Sit down and tell me all about it."

"Are you sure you want to get into this?"

"Of course I want to get into whatever is on your mind so heavy."

Darren rubbed his hands together and looked distant as he said, "Marva, when I met you, I wasn't looking for anybody. I was happy being single, but you came in and turned my world upside down. I tried to ignore it, that's why I didn't even ask for your phone number. But when we ran into each other three times I knew it had to be fate. I just had to see where it would go. Before I met you I chose women for all the wrong reasons and now it feels like I've finally done things right this time."

Marva patted Darren's thigh as he continued.

"I knew a month ago that I had a job offer in Seattle as the Chief In-House Legal Counsel for a Naval Contractor. My job here is outsourcing most of my work to Taiwan and I'll be out of a job if I stay, but I don't want to go to Seattle because I don't want to lose you. What we have is so special that I don't want to take a risk of losing it due to a long distance relationship."

"And that's why you've been a little quieter lately."

"Yes, I've had a lot of things on my mind. How do you choose between a great woman whom you're beginning to fall head over hills with or a great opportunity plus a lucrative salary?"

"Darren, what do you really want to do?"

"In a perfect world, I'd stay with you to see where this relationship leads us. I'd probably sell my place and start my own consulting business and work real hard until I built it into a great success, so you'd be proud of me."

Marva nuzzled up real close to him.

"Baby, why don't you go ahead and sell your house and start your business? You can move in with me and build your business."

"I couldn't impose on you like that. Besides, I don't have a lot of equity in the house. I would probably have to take a loss to sell it."

"Darren, I believe in you. Follow your dream so you won't have any regrets. Besides, I'm falling for you, too."

Darren looked surprised, as he said, "Are you really?"

Marva kissed him and said, "Of course, silly. Look at you, what's not to love?"

He leaned in and kissed her hard, pushing her backwards on the couch.

Marva giggled and said, "You can have the whole basement for your office and we'll make it work."

"Do you really mean that, baby?"

"Of course, I do."

"You've made me the happiest man alive and I'm going to make you proud."

"You already make me proud."

Darren kissed her so hard that she could hardly breathe. He picked her up, took her to the bedroom, and laid her gently on the bed. He stood and looked at her.

"You are so beautiful."

Marva couldn't control the smile that captured her face. She thought about things that some women obsess about before having sex with a man for the first time: what kind of underwear am I wearing, remember to hold your stomach in tightly, and don't be too freaky … things that most men don't even care about. Darren started to undress her and planted a kiss where each button or hook was. He turned her onto her back, kissing her shoulder blades, her neck and the length of her back. He ran his fingers over her naked skin until she trembled with delight. He kissed, and nibbled on her breasts until she felt her body gyrating out of control. Then he kissed her up and down every inch of her body with sweet kisses that felt like misty raindrops on a hot summer's night. He kissed her until he found the center of her joy and alternated pleasuring her with his fingers and his tongue. When her pleasure was about to erupt, he laid her flat on her stomach. He lay on top of her and entered her from behind. With one hand he caressed her clitoris and with the other hand he manipulated her breasts. All the sensations at once were almost too much for her to bear. Her body erupted with passion. Marva could not think of a time when she had been nearly this satisfied or happy. For once, she was the one to roll over and go to sleep. She thought, *Nothing came close to this EVER. Wow, this was worth the wait.*

*****

Trisha opened her salon for Alexis, even though Sunday was her day off. Alexis was one of Trisha's favorite clients and her best tipper. Alexis had been out of the country for six weeks. Her father owned the local Hockey team and had his hands in all things legal and illegal. He owned a bank, a funeral home, several plush clubs and restaurants and had real estate holdings all over the world. For Alexis' birthday, her father purchased a beautiful house in South Shore Harbour and had it professionally decorated. Alexis had it all and Trisha worshipped her. With Alexis' influence, Trisha opened her shop and kept her chair filled with wealthy clients.

Alexis got out of her BMW and walked in, looking as if she had fallen off the pages of Vogue and into a vat of gold, diamonds and other precious stones.

"How was your trip? I love that outfit. You are looking good," Trisha said.

"Thanks girl. Italy was good. I just had to get away. I was just too upset to stay around here another minute."

"Well, what do you have to be depressed about? You are beautiful, well-educated and have more money than Donald Trump and Bill Gates, together."

"You know it had to be man trouble."

"Been there, done that." Putting a cape around Alexis, Trisha said, "Now, tell your hairdresser all about it."

They laughed.

"Well, I went to a cocktail party that my dad gave for his hockey team and I met this tall, good-looking man there. He was articulate, well dressed, and so attentive. He was interesting and intelligent. I didn't want to go to this function, but my dad insisted, you know how that is."

Trisha nodded and said, "Yeah, I know, how that is."

Alexis continued, "After I got there, things were great, I met Lorne and I was so happy! We talked all night, but when he left he didn't even ask for my phone number. I thought I'd never see him again, but a couple of days later, I ran into him at a play in the music hall. Afterwards, we went for ice cream and talked for hours again. But he still didn't ask for my number, so I thought maybe he just wanted to be friends. Then, the next week, I ran into him at a fundraiser. This time we really clicked and he said that since we'd met three times it had to be fate."

Trisha nodded in all the right places and made encouraging remarks as Alexis shared the details of her man woes.

"Lorne wined and dined me and treated me like a real princess. He bought me beautiful gifts, cooked exotic meals, and anticipated my every need. I begged him until he moved into my house and things were going great. We were so happy, I had to stop and pinch myself. It was just unreal."

"Well, honey, that doesn't sound like trouble to me. A man treats you well, buys you great gifts and makes you feel special, what's bad about that?"

"There was nothing bad about it, except my dad doesn't think anyone is good enough for me. So he had Lorne investigated and found out that he is a con man that stalks women, then finds a way into their lives and steals everything he can get his hands on."

Trisha's mouth flew open; she put the hairdryer down and walked around the chair to face Alexis.

"Oh my God, you've got to be kidding? Tell me you are kidding."

"I couldn't believe it, either. So, I went to Arizona to see a woman who had been his victim. I took a picture of him from the surveillance video at my house and she recognized him. I talked to another woman in Vegas and the trail goes on and on. The picture from the surveillance video is the only one of him that exists. None of the other women had any pictures, and neither did I."

"My God, girl. That is awful. I can't believe that he would do something like that."

"I can hardly believe it either and it still hurts."

She held her hand up to her face to wipe a tear when Trisha noticed her bracelet.

"Alexis, that is a beautiful charm bracelet. Where did you get it?"

"Lorne gave it to me. He says the third time is the charm."

Trisha's mouth fell open. "Oh my God! Marva."

*****

Marva fell into a deep sleep. When she woke, Darren was sitting, completely dressed, in a chair across from her bed. When she woke and saw him and recalled the night before, she felt a little shy. He smiled at her.

"Good morning, sleepy head."

At the sound of his voice, she felt a little tingle. She tried to pull up the sheets to cover her nakedness, but he went over to the bed and pulled the covers down.

"Please, don't cover up. You're beautiful and I want to look at you."

Marva felt another blush taking over her body.

"The first night I saw you, Marva, I wanted to touch your skin and feel your hair, but I didn't want my loins to make decisions for me that my mind would regret. I wanted to make sure you were as beautiful on the inside as you are on the outside. In the past, I've made that mistake and chosen women for other reasons."

Darren came and sat next to her on the bed and kissed her slowly and tenderly-- morning breath and all.

Then, he excused himself, saying, "Stay right there, I'll be right back. Don't move."

Marva couldn't help herself. She ran to the bathroom and quickly brushed her teeth, washed her face and applied a little lip-gloss. Darren returned a few minutes later with a tray of freshly cut fruit, a couple of cheese wedges and freshly juiced apple juice. Marva sat up in the bed as he entered the room. He set the tray in her lap and fed her breakfast. Darren kissed her wherever the juicy fruit dripped on her body. Marva giggled and enjoyed every minute of their sensuous breakfast.

"It's a beautiful Sunday. Let's take your car, let the top down and drive up to the coast to get some fresh seafood for dinner," Darren said.

"Of course, but first let's take a bath."

Ever since she'd bought a house with a Jacuzzi for two, she'd dreamed about a steamy bath with a handsome man.

After Alexis left the salon, Trisha paced the floor of her shop, wondering how to tell Marva about what Alexis had told her. After several hours, Trisha decided to call Marva. Trisha got the voicemail at Marva's house and on her cell phone. Trisha left urgent messages on both. Marva ignored both messages, she knew Trisha was jealous and wanted to spoil her fun.

The drive was wonderful; Darren handled her Mercedes expertly around the curvy roads. They chose jumbo shrimp and scallops straight from the fishing boats. The happy couple chatted, sang with the music on the radio and stopped to look in some of the interesting little shops on the way home. They were the envy of people who saw them. On the way back into the city, Darren pulled into the grocery store parking lot and bought everything to prepare dinner.

When they got home, Darren said, "Go relax and put your feet up, dinner will be ready in a few minutes. But before you go, choose the music for dinner."

Marva chose Anita Baker. She decided to check the messages before she changed her clothes. Trisha had called seventeen times, each message sounding more urgent than the next. Marva picked up the phone and called Trisha's number. She answered on the first ring.

"Marva, I've got to talk to you about Darren, I think he might be a conman. I think he used to date a client of mine, Alexis, and she told me how they met. It was the same story of you and Darren. She's going to bring a picture of him by the shop tomorrow. I'm sure it's the same man."

"You just can't stand to see me happy, can you? You've always thought that you were prettier than I was and I should only have your sloppy leftovers. You're just mad that I've found someone to love me and I didn't have to prance around half-naked and show off my store-bought tits and ass to do it. Get over it, Trisha. He chose me--not you. Maybe if you weren't such a little money hungry skank, he--or someone would have chosen you."

"Chosen me? Hell, I don't want him. That cock-eyed fool doesn't do anything for me!"

"He doesn't have to do anything for you. He's my man. And what's your man's name? Oh, sorry, I forgot. You don't have one. All you have is notches on the bedpost."

Trisha wasn't bothered by Marva's words, as they held some element of truth. She only wanted to put all that mess behind and get her friend to understand that she might be in danger.

Marva's voice was getting angrier by the second.

"Trisha, as far as I'm concerned, we are no longer friends. I don't care if we've been friends since third grade. The truth of the matter is that I've always been your friend, but you don't know how to be anybody's friend. Forget you know my address and phone number."

Marva was fuming at the nerve of Trisha. She'd done awful things in the past, but this was the straw that broke the camel's back.

Trisha was stunned. She tried to get a word in, but all she heard was the dial tone, as she felt the cold venom her friend released.

Marva hung up the phone and blocked Trisha's home number, cell phone number, shop numbers and her mother's numbers.

Marva changed into a peach, lace, see-through blouse, which she wore with no bra and white shorts. When she returned to the kitchen, the table was set and Darren was tossing the salad.

"What can I do to help?"

Darren turned and looked her up and down. A slow smile crept across his face. He licked his lips, walked to the table, and pulled out a chair.

"Just sit right here and be my motivation."

He kissed her as she sat. Anita Baker was crooning, "You bring me joy . . ." and Marva thought, *Now that's the damn truth.*

"Baby, dinner was spectacular. I believe you were a gourmet chef in another life."

"At one time, I wanted to be a chef. I was going to enroll in culinary arts school, but my mom said I needed a career that paid more money, so I didn't pursue my dream. So now, I'll just use my talents to feed your every need."

Darren walked over to Marva's chair and pulled it away from the table.

"Dessert will be served on the patio," Darren said.

Darren had turned off the lights so they could see more of the sparking stars from the screened porch. The only visible light came from the crescent moon and stars. Darren positioned Marva on the chaise lounger and went back to the kitchen, returned with two Banana Popsicles in an ice bucket. He broke one in half and gave one stick to Marva and he took the other stick and put it in mouth as he removed Marva's white Keds slip-on shoes. He sucked on the Popsicle as he removed her blouse, shorts and thong underwear.

"Eat your dessert, baby," Darren said.

Darren removed the Popsicle from his mouth and began to rub it gently on Marva's breast, sucking the drippings and alternating between the warm of his mouth and the cold of the

Popsicle. She began to respond and moan with delight as he began to rub her with the Popsicle. He inserted the Popsicle in her and began biting and licking her to pleasure. Her moans turned to whimpers and she tried to sit up because the pleasure was almost unbearable. He held her down on the lounger as her pleasure shook her. Her body went limp and Darren slipped on the lounger next to her and snuggled her close to him.

The next morning, Marva called in to work.

"Are you sick? You sound funny," asked Lynn.

Marva cleared her throat, "Yes, just a little."

She wanted to say, *No, I'm not sick, I've never been happier. I'm calling in because I'm too damn happy to work today.* Darren had left early. He said he had a lot of business to handle. He was going to get a realtor to put his house on the market and tell his manager that he was not taking the job in Seattle.

*****

Monica released her morning class early; Trisha had said it was an absolute emergency that they talk, and that Monica needed to be at her shop at 9:30 am. Monica hurriedly drove to Trisha's salon to find Trisha pacing the floor, waiting for her. The two ladies went to Trisha's office and out of earshot of the other stylists. Alexis arrived as promised, and as she revealed Lorne's picture, Monica let out a gasp. She couldn't believe the story Alexis told.

"What did Marva say when you talked to her?" Monica asked.

"She didn't believe me and she blocked all my numbers, so I can't call her, she thinks I'm just jealous."

"We've got to make her listen."

Trisha and Monica decided to go to Marva's job to talk to her over lunch. When they arrived, they were told that she was home sick. When they arrived at Marva's house, they saw Darren taking boxes out of the car. They decided to wait to talk to Marva alone.

When Darren finished unloading the car, he found Marva outside, cleaning up the sticky mess from the night before. Darren kissed her.

"I would have done that."

"It was my pleasure, today, and it was my pleasure last night."

They both smiled a knowing smile.

"How did it go this morning?" she asked.

Darren looked pained. "Well, I'm officially unemployed and my house is for sale."

Marva took his hand. "It's going to work out just fine. In a few months, you're going to have more clients than you can handle."

"I'll believe that, as long as I have you by my side."

"Well, I'm planning to be right here, cheering you on with my pom-poms." She leaned over and gave him a kiss, and he returned it slow and easy.

"The realtor suggested I leave all the furnishings in tact and just remove my personal items. She thought the house would show better that way. She said the new buyer might want to buy some of the furnishings, especially since most them were specifically designed for that house."

"I agree with her. It is perfectly decorated and I'm sure when people look at it, they'll want to move right in."

"The realtor said the real estate market was slowing a bit and if I sold the furnishings with the house, I might be able to break even and not have to bring money to the closing table."

"Well, why do you look so sad?" Marva asked.

"Because it closes a chapter in my life and starts a new one. With the new one, I'm starting from scratch and that means it might be a few months of struggle before I get my feet planted firmly on the ground. I don't want to struggle with you, I want to give you the best."

"In time you will, baby. Don't worry about that. I struggled all my life to get everything I have, and I'm used to it."

Darren kissed her and hugged her close.

"Next, I have to go car shopping. My car was leased through my company and I have to return it."

"Sweetie, why don't you take my Mercedes? You'll probably need a nice car to go see prospective clients. I can drive the Explorer. It's just sitting there and needs to be driven, anyway. That way, you don't have to worry about that until you start bringing in clients."

Marva thought she saw Darren's eyes mist with tears as he squeezed her hand.

"In fact, Darren, I have an excellent idea. You're going to have to develop a business plan, a networking group and a list of prospective clients. Why don't I help you with those things while we are in Hawaii?"

Darren looked a little puzzled. Marva broke the silence.

"I work for National and I have flight privileges. On certain trips, I can take a companion with me. I have five weeks of vacation left. Why don't we take four or five days to do some planning?" she kissed him between each word, as she continued. "We could do some lovemaking, sightseeing, lovemaking, planning, lovemaking, planning, and sightseeing and did I say lovemaking."

Darren smiled a wide grin. "I can see where that can be profitable to us both. When do we leave?"

"Is seven o'clock tonight early enough?"

"Perfect! That's great, that will give me enough time to get the rest of my things from the house, pack a bag, get some cash and return my car."

He kissed her goodbye and took the keys to the Explorer so he'd have more room to pack his personal items. By 7:00 pm the couple was snuggled, holding hands, in the first-class cabin of flight 1705 heading to Oahu, while Marva's friends were pacing the floor wondering where she was and what to do.

Marva wasn't ready to go when the limousine picked them up in the front of the hotel. Five days of bliss. How could you say goodbye to such a perfect trip with a perfect man, in a perfect place? Marva fully expected to wake up from her dream at any minute. Darren had treated her to all kinds of exotic pleasures all over the island. He touched her lower back and she trembled at his touch.   They reluctantly headed toward the waiting town car and started for the airport.

*****

Darren and Marva sluggishly exited the car.   They were home again and the beauty of Hawaii had been traded for suburbia.   As they approached the front door, they noticed an envelope taped to the lead-glass front door.   Marva recognized Monica's handwriting. It was marked 'urgent'. Marva unlocked the door and went directly to the phone.

"Marva, is everything all right?" Darren asked.

Marva held up one finger and continued to listen to Monica on the phone. When she hung up, she said, "Baby, I need to run over to Monica's for a minute. There's some type of emergency and she's crying and won't talk about it over the phone. I'll be back as soon as I can."

"Do I need to drive you?"

"No, baby. I'll be all right."

"I'll look in the freezer and see what I can whip up for dinner. Call me if you need me."

Marva gave him a quick peck and headed out the door.

When Marva arrived, she noticed Trisha's car in the driveway and a car that looked just like Darren's.   Monica answered the door, and then guided her into the den where the other ladies were assembled.

"Monica, what's going on?" Marva asked.

Alexis started the conversation by handing Marva a picture.

"Marva, do you recognize this man?"

"It looks like my boyfriend, Darren, but it's so blurry it could be anyone."

"I believe this is the man you know as Darren. I knew him as Lorne Blackmon. I met him almost a year ago and had a great relationship with him. He gave me the best sex I ever had and treated me better than any man has ever treated me. I thought he was my soulmate but my father was suspicious of him and had him investigated."

"I don't know what this shit is about, but I'm out of here."

Marva headed toward the door but Alexis stood in front of her, begging her to listen.

"Did Darren tell you the third time is a charm?"

Marva turned to look at this woman.

"Yes, he did. But I also told Monica and Trisha about it, so you jealous bitches probably got together and put this charade together."

"Marva, did you recognize the car outside? Did he cook dinner for you at a house in South Shore Harbour?"

"Yes, but I also told that to Trisha and Monica." Marva's eyes glared. "I don't know what type of game you all are playing, but it is low." Marva turned her attention to Monica.

"I would have expected this type of thing from Trisha, but not you, Monica. What's gotten into you?"

"My love for you, Marva, has gotten into me. You know me. You know us. We've been there for each other like family. We even shared lunches in elementary school when my mom didn't have enough money to buy lunch. Do you think I would jeopardize a friendship of almost thirty-five years just because I am jealous? Marva you know, I've always applauded your successes as if they were my own," Monica said, pleadingly.

Marva was confused; she knew what Monica said was true. Her heart began to soften. But, then, she thought of Darren, who had shown her more love than she had thought possible.

"Monica you know I love you. We've been through a lot together. So, why are you trying to hurt me?"

Monica tried to reason with her. "Marva, I'm not trying to hurt you. I'm trying to keep him from hurting you."

Marva began to walk towards the door, again. Trisha and Monica ran to stop her. As Marva was about to turn the doorknob, Alexis walked up to her and put her perfectly manicured hand on Marva's forearm revealing the identical bracelet and charms.

"What type of Popsicles do you like Marva? Lorne likes banana Popsicles."

All the color left Marva's face. Trisha rushed to her and led her to the couch. Marva sat down and Alexis got on her knees in front of her and held her hands.

"Marva, the house he brought you to was my house. The car he's been driving is my car. We were together for eight blissful months. Last Monday, he took $2,000,000 from my father to never see me again. He also left with some of my jewelry and cash." Marva started to cry and Alexis reached over to give her a tissue.

"Marva, that's not all, Lorne--Darren or whatever his name is, has done similar things to women all over the country," Monica, said.

Alexis began to cry along with Marva.

"My dad was going to kill him, but I begged my dad not to hurt him, I thought maybe I was different to him. I told my dad that Lorne had sex tapes of us and I was afraid they'd get out if anything happened to him. I told him I couldn't live if everybody saw me that way. I know my dad wanted to kill him; but I pleaded for Lorne. I took the information the detective gave my father and went to investigate myself. I talked to Delia in Phoenix, she knew him as Stephen. They were together for a year. She went out of town on business and when she returned, he had taken all of her furniture, expensive art and her Lincoln continental. She said he took more than $350,000 in cash. The worse part about it is there was nothing that she could do about it. The law considered him her common-law husband. He took money from joint accounts, which had money they'd earned while they were together. He also took half the proceeds of the sale of her business. It was all legal. He left divorce papers for her to sign, stating that he was leaving her the house and her limo business and what he had taken was his portion of the settlement."

"I can't believe that."

Alexis continued, "I also went to Vegas to see Natalya. She knew him as Winston. They were together for thirteen months. He was a chef in her restaurant. She says she still loves him, even though he swindled her out of over $1,000,000 that he was supposed to use to start another restaurant. I visited Sidney, in Memphis. They were together for almost two years. I didn't get to talk to her because she'd had a nervous breakdown. Her mom said she believes Grant, as they knew him, got away with close to $3,000,000 from her daughter's trust fund. Most of the women didn't want to pursue charges, either because of the scandal or their love for him."

"What would he want with me? I don't have money like that."

"I can't listen to any more!" Marva was having sharp pains in her stomach. "I can't listen to any more of this."

She sat grasping for air, so Monica made her put head between her knees. Trisha gave her a paper bag to breathe into. When Marva's breathing was normal, Trisha and Monica surrounded her with a hug. Marva sobbed violently, then broke from their grasp.

"I'm going home."

"Sweetheart, what are you going to do?" Monica said.

"I'm not sure."

"We can go with you," Trisha said.

"No, I'll be just fine."

"Please, let me drive you!" Monica insisted.

"No, I'll call you all tomorrow."

Marva sped out of the driveway headed for home.

When she walked in, Darren said, "Perfect timing, dinner is ready. I was about to call and check on you."

Marva stood in the kitchen door way. Darren turned to look at her and noticed the tear stains on her aqua silk blouse.

Her eyes were red and puffy and her hair was wild. Darren went to her and took her in his arms. Marva fought to be free.

Darren said, "Honey, what's wrong? Is Monica okay?"

Marva ignored his questions and fired questions of her own.

"What is your real name?"

Darren looked shocked.

"Marva, what are you talking about."

"It's a simple question. What is your real name?"

Darren looked at her with a puzzled look in his eyes.

"Is your name, Grant, Stephen, Lorne, Winston, or Darren?"

Darren walked to the counter and took a sip from a glass of wine that he had sitting on the counter. He brought the bottle to the table and sat it next to Marva.

"My real name is Darren."

"I just had a conversation with Alexis. She says her house is not up for sale."

"No, it's not, I lied to you. But there is an explanation."

"I'd like to hear it."

"Yes, I have been known by all of the names you mentioned. My father's name was Grant Lorne Stephens and my little brother, who died shortly after birth was christened Winston." He took a sip of the wine and a long deep breath. A heavy palatable sadness fell over him and he looked like a sad little boy. Even in all her own distress Marva wanted to comfort him.

"My father went to New York University. He was a smart man, but he was poor and definitely not business savvy. His brilliance really took his professors by surprise. While attending NYU, was an electrical engineering student who invented several patents that were very lucrative. One was a device similar to what he now call a computer processor. It was part of the genius behind sophisticated calculators. Now, variations of my father's inventions are used in computers, cellular phones and all kinds of small electronics. My father was a trusting man, so he solicited the help of four of his friends that had the wealth, contacts, and status to help him market his inventions to corporations and the general public. However, his friends--or so he thought at the time, stole his work, presented it as their own and made millions and millions of dollars of which my dad got zero. They disgraced him, and wounded him so much that he was a shadow of himself after that. They were already wealthy, yet they begrudged a poor working man his claim to the fortune he deserved. My father died penniless. We couldn't afford to bury him, so he's buried in a pauper's grave with a couple of dozen other people."

Darren opened his wallet, looked inside the lining, and pulled out an old worn photograph; the images were fading away. His jaw began to clench harder and harder.

"This was the picture my father took with his friends, when he made a gentlemen's agreement with them that he thought was going to change his life and put him on the map. He worked for the Transit Authority at night and went to school during the day. All he wanted was to give his kids the good life, the kind of life he'd dreamed of."

Darren put the picture of five grinning men with champagne glasses raised, in front of Marva's face, as he wiped his tears with his forearm. She glanced at it.

"What does this have to do with you swindling money from women all over the world?"

Darren ignored her question.

"Look at them, Marva. They are all smiling and laughing at my father, knowing they had agreed to betray him."

Darren stopped a minute and took a long look at the picture.

"My baby brother died because my father could not afford to take my mother to the hospital, and I lost my mother because she was never same after that."

The tears were rolling down his face, but no sounds were coming from him.

Anger anew was rising up in him. He sat for a minute, and then continued through gritted teeth.

"My father told me about the men who stole my birthright, sold it, and became even wealthier. Not that they needed more money. They were just greedy."

Darren stopped to wipe his nose and get more wine.

"I, too, went to New York University and studied law and business. Then, I tracked down each man my father had named, gathered information on them, and decided to fuck over their children, like they had fucked over my father's children. I took from each of them what should have been mine in the first place. I now have my father's millions back."

"But what about the innocent women you hurt in the process?"

"The sins of the father are visited upon the children. That's what the Bible says."

Darren wiped his tears and, through gritted teeth and muffled sobs, said, "I inflicted pain on them like their fathers had inflicted on my father. My father couldn't afford a good attorney who couldn't be bribed by the millions his enemies had. So, I became the good attorney my father needed and I found a legal way to take back what they stole."

"But, those women didn't even know your father."

"I violated their trust, yes, but I needed to do it to accomplish my goals. Besides, their fathers provided for them a lifestyle that my father couldn't afford to give his family. They had lifetimes of plenty while I had a lifetime of want. They went to private schools while I went to ghetto schools with torn books and bad teachers. I had to fight every day. But I was determined. It made me strong. It made me determined and it made me successful."

"Don't you feel guilty for what've you've done to their lives?"

"No, I did not break any laws. I changed my name legally in each state and I took money from accounts where my name had been added as a partner. I was co-owner of the money. I took property that was legally mine under the state's divorce laws. And I was given money in my hand. I don't have regrets about it. I feel empowered by it. What I took from them is only a fraction of what they took from my father. But, I had the pleasure of fucking them. And nothing is more painful to any man than to have his daughter violated because of him."

"Why me, Darren? My father didn't go to college. In fact, he didn't graduate from high school."

"Marva, this has nothing to do with you. I told you that, with you, I was starting a new chapter in my life. From what I've heard you say, your father was a decent man, and from what I know, he did what he could to provide for his family."

"My father worked in the steel mills all of his life."

"I told you. This has nothing to do with you. You've worked hard, like I did, and you are a self-made woman. I'm with you because I love you. You can ask each of those women. I've done things with and for you that I've never done with any of them. I love you, Marva, and I want to start a life with you. We can start a business that will support you and our children if we chose to have any. I have gotten vengeance from each one of the men who wronged my father. There were four of them and my mission is complete. Now, I can settle down and give all my love to you. That's what I meant when I said, I chose women for other reasons."

Darren reached for Marva's hand.

"I was going to tell you. But I didn't think it was the right time yet. But since it's all out in the open, I need to know if you can live with this? Can you live with me? I need to know because I love you and I don't want to lose you. The big question is, will you be mine?"

He slid off the chair onto one knee and pulled a round diamond solitaire from his pocket.

"I bought it in Hawaii, because I have never met anyone like you. All the other stuff is behind me and I want to build my life with you. Please, Marva make me the happiest man in the world."

The tears fell from her cheek, as she embraced Darren kissed the top of his head.

"Sure, I'll be your wife."

*****

The phone woke Marva from a sound sleep. It was Trisha and Monica on a conference call.

"Marva, how are you? We've been worried about you," Monica said.

Marva propped herself up on her elbow. "I'm fine."

Darren nuzzled her ear.

"I appreciate your concern, but Darren and I are just fine. We got engaged last night."

"Marva have you gone completely stupid? That man is a con artist," Trisha said.

Marva's temper began to boil,

"Again, as I said, thank you for your concern, but I will not have you talk about the man I am going to marry in that way. Darren did what he did for very good reasons. He didn't break any laws and he is going to be my husband, so the two of you had better get used to it."

Darren took Marva's hand and put it on his swollen penis as he began to nibble on her breast. Marva squirmed.

"Good day, ladies. I have some business to take care of." She replaced the receiver to the cradle and turned her attention to Darren.

The wedding was beautiful. They decided to go back to Hawaii and have a small ceremony on the beach. Trisha and Monica were absent, but Marva hardly noticed. After the honeymoon, they returned to pack up the house. Marva got a job transfer and she and Darren moved to Seattle, after all.

On their fifth anniversary, Marva's divorce papers were delivered to her door while she was getting ready for their extravagant anniversary party. She found, taped to the mirror, withdrawal slips indicating that Darren had emptied all their joint accounts. According to him, it was roughly half of the marital assets, and if she objected, he would attach her 401K and her thrift plan from the airline, in addition to making the divorce a public battle. Darren had gotten all the men who'd wronged his father. But, he hadn't gotten revenge on Marva's mother, the woman his father had been with the night his brother died. He'd wondered if Marva could be his half sister, because of the birthmark on her left buttock.

1. Marva should
   A. Spend everything she has to track Darren down.
   B. Find a way to reconcile with her husband.
   C. Cut her losses and move on with her life.

2. Marva should
   A. Make every attempt to expose Darren as a con man.
   B. Try to find a way to get through the divorce.
   C. Try to care for her own emotional and mental health.

3. Marva should blame
   A. Darren.
   B. The men who stole from Darren's father.
   C. Herself.

4. Marva should attempt to
   A. Get all the money back from Darren.
   B. Split their acquired assets 50/50.
   C. Realize that money is the least of her worries.

5. Marva should
   A. Move on and let the chips fall where they may.
   B. Try to keep things quiet to minimize the social damage.
   C. Make her life public to warn other women and embarrass Darren.

6. Marva should
   A. Search for ways to get revenge on Darren.
   B. Pray he comes home.

C.   Search for ways to build her self-esteem.

7.   Marva should

A.   Feel like a fool.

B.   Feel abused.

C.   Feel like she got what she deserved.

8.   Marva's marriage was

A.   A façade.

B.   Real in every sense.

C.   Destined for disaster.

9.   Marva should

A.   Fight hard against the divorce and make him face her.

B.   Accept the divorce, only if there is a fair distribution of assets.

C.   Sign the papers and bow out gracefully.

10.   Marva should

A.   Try to quickly find a new husband.

B.   Give up on love.

C.   Try to heal and forgive herself.

11.   Marva should

A.   Call Darren's mother.

B.   Realize her mother is to blame for all of this.

C.   Seek counseling.

12.   Marva should

A.   Legally fight Darren and beat him at his own game.

B.   Find Darren and make him tell her to her face that he wants a divorce.

     C.   Gather the women who have been hurt by Darren and form a plan to extract revenge.

13.   Marva should

     A.   Find where Darren has stashed his money and steal it from him.

     B.   Only be concerned about the fair and equitable distribution of community assets.

     C.   Forget about the money and start over.

14.   Marva should

     A.   Hire a hit man to kill Darren.

     B.   Pray for Darren.

     C.   Forget Darren and move on with her life.

15.   Marva should

     A.   Track down Darren's family and get revenge.

     B.   Ask her mother to apologize so Darren will come home.

     C.   Ask her friends to forgive her.

If your answers total

    Mostly A's read ending X

    Mostly B's read ending Y

    Mostly C's read ending Z

Ending X

Marva sat at her dressing table and looked at the scraps of paper that meant her life was over. How could just a few pieces of paper change her life so drastically? Yesterday, she had been cuddling with her husband and watching Frazier and, now she was another victim of a vengeful man. She had guests who were supposed to start arriving in a couple of hours. How would she face them? What excuse would she give for the absence of her husband at such an important event? Congressmen were on the guest list, along with-well known celebrities and business people. Their business had been extremely successful and they were known in all the right social circles. This sandal could ruin her. But she wouldn't let it.

"I'm not going down like this," Marva growled.

A powerful, but controlled, anger rose out of her. It kept her focused. She knew she had a party to throw and there was no time to break down. Marva finished dressing in the gown her designers had been working on for four months. The beadwork alone had taken more than two months to complete. She made her grand entrance at the appropriate time and gathered the blossoming crowd's attention. She spoke clearly and convincingly, "Thank you for coming on this occasion. This was the speech that my husband was supposed to make, but there has been an extreme emergency at our facility in Florida and he was forced to go attend to it. Hopefully, he'll be back before the evening is over. I know you're disappointed, and so am I, but the party shall go on. I stayed behind to celebrate with all of you, so let's get this party started."

Standing on the balcony overlooking their five- acre estate with its own private lake she raised her arm and beautiful fireworks were released. The crowd oohed and aahed.

Marva mixed and mingled all night, making all the guests feel welcome. She was gracious and attentive and when she was with someone they never felt as if her attention was divided. Marva managed to greet each guest individually and thank him or her for coming. The night was a perfect success. She had seen to every detail and things had come off without a hitch-- except for the no husband, at her anniversary party. Marva made her way back to her bedroom and started a bath. She eased her aching body into the hot water, wanting to get her cry out. But no tears ever came.

"I guess I'll have to plan a pity party some other time. I have too much to do," Marva said, rising from the now cold water.

She woke from a fitful sleep at five a.m. eager to get her plans rolling. There were so many ideas that they were running around in her head and bumping into one another. Then she reached for the phone and listened to the groggy voice that answered on the other end of the line.

"Do you know what time it is?" asked Russell, Marva's attorney and friend.

"I told you to stop with the champagne last night," Marva replied.

"Marva, what do you want this early in the morning? Can I call you back after ten?"

"No, Russell. I need to speak to you immediately. Meet me at your office in one hour. I have to speak with you, NOW, Russell."

He heard the determination in her voice but tried one more time for additional sleep.

"Marva, is this really important?"

"Russell, get up. I'm going to wait on the phone until you are out of bed. One hour in your office, please."

This time he heard something in her voice that spoke of desperation. It told him that his friend needed him.

When Russell arrived, Marva was sitting out front waiting on him. Her hair was still up in the same hairdo as she'd worn at the party. It looked a little funny with her warm-up suit and athletic shoes. She smiled at him, but he knew it was forced. Russell busied himself turning on lights, air conditioning, and computers. When those tasks were completed, he sat in his big black leather chair and turned to face Marva.

Looking at him sitting there almost made Marva laugh. The chair made him look like a stuffed sausage. But, her next thought kept her from laughing, *His brain is stuffed with knowledge that has saved me time and time again.* And that was what she needed.

"Now, will you tell me why you dragged by ass out of bed this early on a Sunday morning?"

"I want you to take a look at these."

"Marva, those are divorce papers," Russell said with a puzzled look on his face.

"Yes, Russell. It doesn't take a rocket scientist to figure that out."

Russell read the papers. After every few sentences, he'd look at Marva with questioning eyes. Marva knew she'd have to tell him the whole story, eventually. But she wanted to work on a need to know basis for the time being.

"Is there a mistake or loop hole or anything out of order? Is all of this legal?"

"From what I can see your husband has dotted every 'I' and crossed every 'T'" Russell said, slowly examining all the documents.

"So it is legal for him to take all the liquid assets and leave me with only paper assets?"

"Well, yes and no. Yes, in that from the looks of it he left you with half."

"But the bad half …with a $22,000 a month mortgage and another $6,000 a month in upkeep. And he's left me the goodwill portion of the business with no money to run it."

"Marva, it looks that way, but the 'no' part of it, is that it can be fought in court and you'd have a good case. The problem is you'd be forced to air your dirty laundry in public."

"No, Russell, I don't want my life to be all over the news."

"Marva, do you want to explain to me what's going on here? I thought you two were the happy couple to be envied by all."

"I thought so too, but I was wrong."

"When did this happen?"

"Last night, the coward, left these papers on my dressing table, before the party."

"He was very thorough in his plans. The only thing that would save you would be if there was a child involved."

Marva sat up attentively, a new plan forming in her mind.

"Gotcha." A new smile crossed her face and Russell could tell this one was for real. Marva and Russell made plans for temporary financing for the business and the household.

Marva left Russell and decided to take a quick run around the lake. It was still early, so she waited in her car in front of the drug store until it opened. She opened a new Aretha Franklin CD and listened to the words, finding a song that spoke to her heart. She turned the volume up and began bobbing her head like a teenager, singing the words,

"Everybody is somebody's fool."

A few months ago, she'd decided to stop her birth control and she didn't tell Darren because she knew what he would say. At forty-six, she felt getting pregnant had to be now or never and Darren had always had one more goal he needed to accomplish before he thought it was time. She had begun to notice how tender her breasts were and she had been too busy with the party to realize how late she was. She decided to go the drug store and get a pregnancy test. After about fifteen minutes of waiting, the manager unlocked the store. Marva went in and purchased several pregnancy tests.

Marva knew there was no such thing as a perfect crime, so she set out to find Darren's mistakes. She went through his papers in his office and found an empty note pad near the phone. She scratched on it with a pencil until the indentations on the pad showed up. It read 'SEA 1708—9:55 BLZ 1:45." She thought it looked like an airline reservation. With a brief investigation, she discovered that Darren was leaving Seattle going to Belize. That was all she needed to know. With her contacts at the airline, Marva was able to find a confirmation of Darren's one-way ticket to Belize. This was the break she needed.

Marva asked Russell to hire a detective to trace Darren's whereabouts as she geared up for the fight of her life. She thought, *The other women you swindled were rich girls who were not used to fighting for what they got, but I had to fight for everything, and I'm not going to take this one lying down.* She smiled, knowing that she'd be face to face with her husband very soon.

"You hurt the wrong one, baby," she said with a wicked chuckle and a determined smile on her face.

Marva was sleeping and dreaming peacefully when she got the sudden urge to run to the bathroom. It was as if her bladder would burst. She decided to take the pregnancy test, even though she already knew what the results would be.

Later that day, she went to see her doctor, and called Russell as soon as she left.

"Russell, what was that you were telling me about a child changing the whole scenario of Darren's plans?" Marva asked, as soon as she heard his voice.

"Well, a child has to be kept in the style that the child has been accustomed to living. Also, the child could be appointed a special attorney to investigate the estate and, with that, there could be a more equitable distribution of the liquid estate based on the child's needs. But there's no heir to give us that type of leverage."

"Oh, but there is now," Marva said with a high pitched shrill in her voice. "Be the first to congratulate me on the baby."

"Marva, what are you talking about?"

"Russell, I'm just leaving my doctor's office and it appears that I am indeed with child."

"Darren's child?"

"Of course, Darren's child!"

"Marva, how could that be? Have you seen him?"

"Rus, you don't want to know! Believe me."

"Well, I guess it's don't ask, don't tell." They both laughed.

"We are back in the ball game. Make sure to take care of yourself. We need to get sonogram pictures and . . ."

"I'm holding them, now. Oh, by the way, Russell, did I tell you I'll be having twins?"

Russell dropped the phone. He couldn't believe her luck.

*****

Darren walked along the private beach in Belize, trying to determine, where he was going to build his house. There were several beautiful spots and the land was cheap. He chose a peak with an eastern exposure that would maximize the sunlight and provide a panoramic view.

When he drove up to his rented condo, he noticed a black car parked in his driveway with two men sitting inside. When he approached, the men exited the car on both sides, and the big one asked, "Darren Saunders?"

"Yes, may I help you?"

The man pulled a thick envelope from his coat pocket and said, "You've been served." Both men immediately returned to their vehicle and left. Darren opened the envelope as he mounted the steps. On top of the legal papers, was a note from Marva.

> *"Hi Honey, just wanted to let you know that your soon-to-be-born kids and I miss you very much. It pained me to have to freeze all of your funds, but you'll understand after you read the enclosed documents. Looking forward to seeing you soon.*
>
> *Love,*
>
> *Your Wife and Unborn Children."*

Darren sat down and read all the papers. He scratched his head. What could she be planning? He was sure that she couldn't be pregnant, she had been on birth control.

They'd discussed starting to try to have children but had decided the timing wasn't right.

Darren could not believe his eyes when he returned to Seattle for the divorce hearing. He saw Marva sitting across from him in the judge's chambers, smiling, with her huge pregnant stomach. He knew the baby couldn't be his but he wasn't sure what she was trying to pull. Darren said, "Your honor, I move that these proceeding be postponed until the birth of the child."

Marva interrupted, "Children."

The judge agreed and ordered DNA tests upon delivery of the children.

Marva took excellent care of herself and her unborn children. Regardless of how or why they had been conceived, the twins were her children and she loved them. They were not due for another three weeks when she began to have labor pains. Russell took her to the hospital and Marva delivered a healthy boy weighing in at 5 lbs. 9 oz. and a beautiful baby girl weighing 4lbs. 1 oz.

Darren couldn't believe the DNA results of 99.7 and 99.4. He had the test redone three times and still was not convinced until he visited his son and saw the family birthmark on him. The joy he felt surprised him, their tiny little feet and hands amazed him and filled his heart with an unspeakable pride. He didn't think it was possible to love anyone or anything as much as he loved his children.

Darren longed to hold his children. He finally had what he'd always wanted, but it wasn't his. He'd loved Marva, but he had a job to do. Now, she was the mother of his children … the ones he'd always wanted. Marva would not consider his pleas for reconciliation and the judge awarded her the majority of the fortune Darren had thought was secure.

Marva looked beautiful in the beige beaded gown as she walked down the aisle. Her children were with her: Ashley was her flower girl and Ashton was the ring bearer. Trisha, Monica and Alexis were her bridesmaids and Russell had turned out to be the lover she needed. Darren got a chance to see his children grow in photos and short supervised visits. The family he had always wanted was so close and yet, still so far away.

Ending Y

Marva was not surprised by Darren's actions. She had felt a change in him for months. Luckily, she had followed her hunch and set up a high tech surveillance system.

She was aware that he was siphoning off money from the company, but he didn't know about the accounts where the real profits were stashed. He'd managed to take over ten million dollars, but that was only a drop in the bucket for the wealth that they had amassed. The Internet portion of the business, which was Marva's baby, was outselling the brick and mortar stores, but Darren took little interest in it. Transcripts of his phone calls, e-mails and written correspondence kept her apprised of his actions. Marva had added software to his computer that recorded his every key stroke. That information was crucial in her ability to discover his accounts and passwords. It would be a couple of days before he figured out his numbered offshore accounts had been emptied.

As a result of the surveillance Marva managed to find out where he'd stashed the money from his other victims. Her suspicions had been raised when she looked at the house's architectural drawings. While examining the drawings and looking for the most practical space for a new home office, she discovered a small area on the third floor that she had not known existed. It took a couple of days for her to find the entrance, but it paid off.

Inside, she found Darren's diary, which made for interesting reading. In it she discovered his turmoil, the promise he'd made to his mother, his true feelings about her and his future plans. His journals read better than any Sidney Sheldon novel. He poured out his feelings, hopes, dreams and his inner chaos in great detail. He said he loved Marva, but felt he needed to right the wrongs done to his family. When Marva called her mother to ask about her affair, her mother was stunned. She didn't admit to anything, but didn't deny it, either. Darren's little room held many secrets-- including his new identity and passport.

Marva was crushed. She loved Darren, but refused to be his next victim. Even though she knew what Darren was planning, the cruelty of the timing was what hurt the most. Sitting at her dressing table, looking at the pages he'd left behind was almost too much to bear. She ran into his make shift office, only to find it empty. She sat there for the longest time, until a crash downstairs brought her back to reality. She went to see the source of the trouble and realized the maze of activity going on in the house. The florist was putting last minute touches on the entryway arrangement. The caterer was shouting instructions and reprimands in Spanish to the wait staff. The party coordinators were going over details and testing their two-way pagers. The valets were sitting by the front door in two chairs brought from the pool. There had to be at least thirty strangers in her house, but at that moment she felt closer to them than the man she'd shared her life and bed with. Marva sat on the steps with her head in her hands, knowing it was too late to cancel the party; there were less than two hours before the festivities were to begin.

"Marva! Marva! Wake up child. What are you doing sitting down here?"

"I don't know, mom."

Her mom came closer and sat on the steps next to her. When her Mom took her daughter's face in her hand, she noticed the tears running down her face.

"Baby what's wrong? This is supposed to be a happy occasion. What's wrong?"

Marva got up and headed upstairs, with her mother following behind. She handed her mother the letter from Darren.

"Oh, my God! No! I can't believe this. This has got to be some kind of sick joke. Sweetheart, I'm so sorry."

Marva's tears were flowing uncontrollably now. Her mom walked into the bathroom and came out with a cold moist white hand towel.

"Stop it, Marva! Wipe your eyes and stop that crying! Stop it! Do you hear me? Stop the damn crying. You haven't done anything wrong."

"But Mom, I'm so foolish. I knew he'd done things like this in the past."

"Sweetheart, this is not your fault. All you're guilty of is loving a man."

"But, I'm such a fool. I believed him, when he said he loved me. And all the time. . ."

"Marva, we will have plenty of time to work through this. But for now, you have to get ready for this party."

"I can't have a party now! How can I face all these people?"

"I raised you to be strong, to handle the hard stuff like a champion and this is hard stuff, but you can handle it. Now, you're going to stop that crying, get off your ass and go in there and put on that damn gorgeous dress. Put on your make-up, go out there and meet and greet every guest with a smile on your face, even if it kills you. You're not going to let Darren or NO man turn you into a sniffing idiot. Where's the woman I raised? You never let them see you sweat. That's our motto. Remember?"

Marva sat on the bed looking at her mom; surely she didn't understand what she had read. How could she try to make her face all those people?

"Mom, you don't get it. This is my anniversary party, and I have no husband. He's divorcing me. What is there to celebrate? The marriage is over! Once you get a divorce you don't continue to have anniversary parties."

"Marva Ann Danzy! Get in there and get dressed! This has nothing to do with a divorce; he could have divorced you any time. This is about embarrassing you and making you feel small and inadequate. He can divorce you, yes. But he can't take your dignity unless you let him. Some men, who don't feel good about themselves, have to make themselves feel good, by making other people feel bad. And I will not allow you to let him win."

"Mom, but how do I explain his absence? You're supposed to have your husband at an anniversary party."

"Sweetheart, there will be a couple of hundred people here. He could be lost in the crowd. He could be in the bathroom for heaven's sake."

"What about the toast he is supposed to make?"

"I'll make it for him, and tell the guests that he has the stomach flu and can't come out of the bathroom."

"Mom, do you think it'll work?"

"Of course it will," Marva's mom said stroking her daughter's long smooth hair.

With a kiss from her mother, Marva headed for the bathroom.

Marva looked stunning as she descended the spiral staircase. Her guests let out an audible sigh at the sight of her. The transformation was magnificent. The beads on her dress caught the light from every angle. Russell, always nearby, reached for her elbow as she stood on the landing.

The party was a smash. After making the first three or four excuses for Darren's absence, Marva began to believe her own lie.

"Darren came home after eating something that disagreed with him. Dr. Young gave him a prescription and I sent him to bed for a quick nap. He'll be down later."

The words rolled off Marva's lips in such a believable fashion that there seemed to be no suspicions raised; she wouldn't be in the morning's gossip column after all.

*****

Darren tossed and turned in his hotel room bed. He loved his wife, but what did love really have to do with it? He thought, *It's all about the money and ain't a damn thang funny.* Those words had been the lyrics of a song that his dad always played for him as a child. This was to be his last score to settle for his father; now he could live his own life. Marva was a score to settle, but there was something about Marva that got under his skin. She could read him like a book and always seemed to know what he needed. At his lowest points, she could make him laugh. She was so smart that he never got bored with her. She re-invented herself everyday and he always wondered how she would pleasantly surprise him. He craved her mind and body. The smell of her early in the morning, her insatiable sexual appetite, the sound of her love noises almost drove him insane. She knew how to please him and always wanted to try something new and different. He had never desired another woman after being with her. Usually, Darren was ready, when it came time for him to take the money and run, but this time his heart and his head didn't want him to go. He got up, walked around the room, and stood with his back against the wall, trying to sort things out. *He needed to disappear. He wanted his wife. What was she doing?* Was she in tears over the way he'd left things? He was knocking his head against the wall, hoping to free the haze rolling around in his brain. He picked up the phone, but after holding it for several minutes he hung up a couple of times at the sound of the recorded voice that said. *"If you'd like to make a call, please hang up and try your call again. If you need help hang up and dial your operator."*

After several attempts Darren made his call.

"Mom, how are you feeling?"

"I'm fine honey, is that you?"

"Yes mom, it's me."

"Oh, honey it's so good to hear your voice. Are you keeping dry and eating enough? You know it's very important to eat right and always wear good shoes with thick socks. You know your feet are the most important thing on your body. They carry you places. And make sure, you eat something green everyday . . . "

"I know, mom. I know. I have to tell you something."

"Okay, honey mommy's listening."

"Mom, I did it."

"You did what?"

"I got them all. All the men that stole daddy's invention." Silence followed.

"Mom, are you there?"

"Yeah, honey. What do you mean you got them?"

"I tracked each one of them down and I did to their families what they did to ours. And I got our money back, over twenty-five million to be exact. I even got the woman dad was with the night Winston died."

"Honey, what exactly did you do? Oh, my Lord did you kill anybody?"

"No, mom everything I did was legal. I did it through the courts . . ."

"Why honey? Why did you do that?"

"Mom, I told you I would get them back. I promised you . . ."

"Darren, you were just a little boy. I didn't expect you to keep that promise, and besides, I've forgiven those men. I pray for them. Vengeance belongs to God, Darren and that poor woman was just looking for what everybody else was looking for. Just a way to make it through the night."

"But, mom they stole from us and made our life hard. That's why dad died so young . . ."

"Boy, hush up and listen to me. Your dad died because he let hatred consume him. He died because he gave up on himself and he wanted all that money for the wrong reasons. They stole from him, but they didn't steal his brain. He could have made a better living and even made other inventions, but he got stuck in a hate place and the hate killed him."

"No mom, he died because he didn't find justice."

"Did you find justice, Darren? Your father is still dead. That twenty-five million dollars can't bring him back. Darren, you can't be controlled by hate, baby. Love is what keeps this world moving along. God makes wrong things right. If they don't get it in this world, hell is where they will lift their eyes."

"Mom, I don't want to hear about all that heaven stuff!"

"That heaven stuff is what separates us from the animals, Darren. All the money in the world can't make an unhappy man happy. If it weren't for those men, your daddy would have found something else to hate. He was unhappy with himself and that's all to it. And as for that woman, we cleared the air years ago. She didn't know your father was married. He lied to her. She was a victim, just like me."

"But, do you know what they took from us?"

"Did they steal my love for you, Darren? Didn't you always have a roof over your head? Was your stomach ever hungry? No one can steal the love and that's all that matters. Boy, you go and make things right with your wife. Now, I said. Do it NOW!"

Darren sat with his head in his hands, discouraged. He'd thought his mom would be happy.

At Marva's house, the party was going great. Marva mixed and mingled with the guests, making sure that she made everyone feel welcome and attended to. After almost two hours of mingling, smiling and taking pictures, her calm happy exterior was beginning to crack. Her mom, sensing the tension, pulled her daughter away from the guests and gave her a pep talk. As mother and daughter were descending the steps after their chat a familiar voice was heard and they looked to see Darren standing half way up the staircase.

Darren and Marva made eye contact

"Baby, can you join me here?" he asked.

Marva was frozen at the sight of him. He had to ask her again.

"Marva, baby please come here?"

Marva seemed to glide down the steps, and standing together, they looked like perfection. Marva leaned over and kissed Darren the way a woman kisses the man she loves in private. The kiss was so hungry Darren had to pull himself away. The crowd applauded.

"Ladies and Gentleman," Darren spoke. "I'd like to take this opportunity to thank you for witnessing the happiest day of my life. I have been fortunate enough to spend the last five years of my life with the most beautiful woman in the world. I love her with all my heart. I ask God and my wife to please give us at least fifty years together, and then I'll know that heaven really can be here on earth. Please raise your glasses to my wife."

Marva melted into his arms, as the crowd applauded.

Their sixth anniversary was quiet, and after a year of counseling and candid conversations, they knew they would make the other forty-nine years together.

Ending Z

Marva sat among all her beautiful things. She ran her hand across the one thousand thread count Egyptian cotton sheets. Picking up the beautiful monogrammed pillow case, she smelled it for her husband's scent; the scent that started her heart every morning. She'd had everything any woman could ever dream of or imagine, but now it was gone. Marva was too devastated to cry. Within three hours, all of her and Darren's friends, co-workers and neighbors would be arriving at her house. The decorations were in place, the food was prepared, the flowers were scenting the house, but there was no Darren, he wasn't coming home and he wanted a divorce. She couldn't face the guests and well-wishers. Marva's personal assistant looked at her with questioning eyes as she told her to call the people on the guest list and cancel the party. Marva told the caterer to pack up the food and take it to the local homeless shelter to feed the residents. The flowers were to be taken to a geriatric care facility.

Marva thanked the staff, and told them that there had been a family emergency. She packed her small Gucci suitcase and headed for the airport. Marva wasn't sure where she would go, but she knew she had to get out of that house; the 7300 square feet were closing in on her. She pulled out her cell phone and called a familiar number, even though she hadn't dialed it in over five years, it still roamed around in her head. She let it ring once, thought better of the call and then hung up.

As she was about to make another call, the phone rang, and Marva heard Monica's voice.

"Hello, this is Monica Livingston. Did you just try to call me?"

Marva held the phone for a second, not knowing what to say.

"Yeah, . . . Monica I called by mistake. I'm sorry."

"Even if it was a mistake, it's really good to hear your voice. I've really missed you," Monica said.

"I've missed you too, Monica."

"How is life treating you?"

The question caught Marva by surprise. "Fine, everything is fine," Marva lied.

"Well, you won't believe this news, Trisha is seven months pregnant!"

"You've got to be kidding?"

"No, it's for real, she's pregnant... glow and all. She gained forty pounds and is loving it."

"Wow, I didn't think I'd ever live to see this day."

"Marva, are you okay? You sound funny?"

After a long silence and a failed attempt to push back the tears, Marva said, "No, as a matter of fact, nothing is right. You all were right about Darren. He left me, taking most of the money with him. We had a big anniversary party planned and he left me with over 100 guests on the way . . ."

"Oh, Sweetie, I'm so sorry. I hoped we were wrong about him. Is there anything I can do? Where are you? Is there someone with you?"

"I just took off, I'm at the airport."

"Where are you heading?"

"I don't know. I just need to get way. I couldn't stay in that house another minute."

"Come here. I'll pick you up at the airport and you can get to see Trisha and everyone. We've all missed you so."

"Okay," Marva replied. "

"I'll have to check the schedule. I'll call you when I arrive."

Marva arrived to find her friends waiting for her. She melted into Monica's arm. The reunion was bittersweet. Trisha had found love at last, with the UPS man, and they were blissfully happy. Alexis had married a professional hockey player from her father's team. And Monica was now a tenured professor at the local university. Monica encouraged Marva to write about her life with Darren. They all said under the circumstances, they would have done the same thing.

Marva turned her pain into the pages of her journal and with Monica's encouragement she sent it to an agent friend and it became a bestseller and a made for TV Lifetime movie.

Sherese

Sherese looked out her twelfth story office window, checked the weather and decided to leave her coat behind. It was one of those days that reminded her of some vision captured through a photographer's lens or an artist's brush. The sky was a million shades of blue and the sun shone as if it were smiling and blessing everything in its path. The Mexican Hat Dance ring of her cell phone moved her attention from the view outside. Sherese checked the caller ID before she answered the phone.

"Hey Girl, what's up?" came the jubilant greeting from her best friend Lyndsey.

"Hey, Chickie. I was on my way out the door."

"I just wanted to see if you wanted to go to The Pit for lunch today. I feel like BBQ ribs."

"Sorry, Girl. I can't go. I have an interview. I applied for a job at the Houston Chronicle."

"What do you mean you applied for a job? Are you thinking about leaving Oil Unlimited?" asked Lyndsey.

"No, girl I'm not thinking about leaving. I've got benefits and I'm vested in the retirement plan. This is just a part-time job throwing a paper route before I come to work in the morning."

"But, Sherese you already have two jobs. What are you trying to do? Work yourself to death?"

"No. This will only take about an hour or two a day, but the pay is good. And I can still work at Oil Unlimited and Macy's part-time."

Lynsey couldn't resist. "Sherese, that makes no damn sense. Why would you want to work three jobs? Why don't you make that husband of yours get a job? Then you could take a moment to relax for a change. Sherese, Steve needs to get a job and you need to stop letting him take advantage of you."

Sherese took a deep breath and counted to ten to try to control her temper, but before she could stop them, the words flew out. "Why don't you try to get a husband before you criticize mine? At least I have one!"

"You call a man who has sat at home all day for the last three or four years and refuses to work a husband? I call that a burden and I wouldn't want one like that. I believe a man should work to support his family. What kind of man sits home and lets his wife work three jobs?"

"I'm going to hang up, now, before I really curse your ass out. Maybe if you took some time to mind your own business you could get a man and stop complaining about mine."

Lynsey started to reply, but she heard the dial tone. She called Marilyn, the third of their usual threesome. They decided to go to The Pit and pick up something to eat at the park.

"Where is Sherese?" asked Marilyn.

"Sherese is gone on an interview. She wants a third job throwing newspapers in the morning before she comes to work."

Marilyn shook her head. "I hope Steve sells his book before she works herself to death."

"I wonder what kind of insurance policy he has on her."

"Lynsey, don't say things like that!"

"She needs to get rid of that zero! All Steve does is sit home and smoke pot all day. Sherese claims he is writing a book, but it's been nearly three and a half years and he hasn't produced anything other than one get rich scheme after another."

"Remember when he was going to make a million dollars buying real estate with no money down? Then it was Amway. Then he was going to buy items from a catalog for little or nothing then resell them for a huge profit. Everyday, it was something new and Sherese is always standing there like a moron, cheering his ignorant ass on."

Lyndsey, wiping BBQ sauce from her mouth, said, "Can you believe he won't even take the kids to school? He told Sherese that it broke his morning concentration to get his ass up and drop the kids off at school. And he gets too caught up in his work to remember to pick them up so Sherese's mother goes to get them and keeps them until Sherese gets off. Can you believe she is talking about getting another job?"

"No, I can't. I'm not sure how she makes it with the two she has."

Lysney added, "She told me that she cooks, cleans, and washes all day Sunday. She cooks three to four entrees, two or three vegetables, and freezes them so he will have food during the week."

"I know. I went over there to take her some clothes I altered for little Autumn and she had spaghetti, meatloaf, and chicken on the stove at the same time. All the kitchen burners were going and she'd bought this thing that looks like a hotplate; it plugs into the wall gives her two other burners. She had broccoli on one and corn on the other and she was whipping up a big bowl of mashed potatoes. And, I bet you can't guess what he was doing."

"Picking his nose?" laughed Lindsey.

"That too, while he sat at the computer playing solitaire. He yelled in the kitchen for her not to forget to make some gravy, and at that point, I had to get up and leave. I wonder how she is going to fit this new job into her schedule."

"She is going to do it before she comes to work. I guess she'll just not go to bed and work around the clock. It's all too much for me to think about. I have trouble rolling out of bed at six o'clock. I'm late almost every morning. I'm just glad that my supervisor is usually later than I am. Well, enough about crazy people. Speaking of late, we're going to be late getting back to work," Lynsey said, eating her last bite of corn.

Sherese was about to hang up after the fourth ring when Steve answered.

"Hey, Honey, I just called to tell you that I got the job," Sherese said.

"Well, that's good news. Now, maybe we'll have some money sometimes," said Steve.

Sherese was excited at the possibility of having enough money to take a vacation or splurge on a nice dinner or something. Now that she had the job, she had to fit it into her schedule. *I'll pick up the papers at 5:00 am. That means I need to be up by 4: am. I can be dressed and ready to leave at 4:45. I can make my deliveries from 5am to 6:30. I have to cover a 10-mile radius with 107 customers. Tonight, I'll stay up and map out my route,* she thought. *"I'll tell Tom I'll be in late tomorrow to give myself enough time to do my first run through.*

The job was more tiring than she had thought. By the time she got home at around 10:00 pm, put the kids to bed, and fixed lunches, it was after 11:00. Then, she had to be up again at 4:00 am. After a month of this schedule, she was absolutely exhausted.

One Sunday morning, she couldn't wake up. Steve had gone to play golf and the kids were watching cartoons and eating dry cereal from the box on the bed beside her. She kept willing herself to wake up, but her body would not cooperate.

Autumn called her grandmother. "Mommy's sick. She won't get out of bed. Can you come over?"

When the grandmother arrived, Sherese lied and said she was coming down with the flu. Her mom took the kids and told her she would keep them since tomorrow was a federal holiday and school was out. Sherese mustered up enough energy to kiss them goodbye. She thought, *Steve can eat leftovers and I will cook after my paper route in the morning.* Sherese was much too tired to think about moving. She settled into a deep sleep. When she woke, it was 5:00 am and she realized she had slept all of Sunday away. She dressed and hurried off for her route. She was still tired; it was as if all the sleep she'd gotten was still not enough. The route went by quickly; it was a holiday and traffic was light.

When she walked back into the house, she looked through the glass of the double French doors and into her husband's office. He was sitting in a chair with his feet on the desk. His back was to the door and he was on the telephone.

"Now, you know I love you, but I can't. She's off today," Sherese heard him say in a hushed voice. She walked closer. He turned to look at her and said, "I'll be off in a minute."

He returned to the phone call and said, "No, mom, I have a lot of work to do. I'm sure we'll get down with the kids soon. I know they are getting big, but Sherese is working and they have school. It's hard to get away, even if it is only a two hour drive."

Sherese could have sworn she heard a dial tone as she walked closer.

"Listen mom, I'll call you later." He turned to Sherese and said, "I'm glad you're here. You can cook me a decent breakfast, for a change."

Sherese kissed his forehead. "Okay." She went off to change her clothes. The phone call had unsettled her. After she had changed her clothes, she picked up the phone, and then pushed *69 to see where the last phone call had come from.

She didn't know that Steve had suspected she would do this, so he had quickly called his mom, claiming that he thought the phone was out of her, and asked her to call him right back.

Steve had answered the ring with a quick, 'Thanks, mom. I'll call you when we get the phone taken care of."

Now, Sherese heard the familiar number recited by the mechanical voice. She felt almost guilty. *Why am I tripping? Steve was talking to his crazy mama.*

Sherese went downstairs and cooked all of Steve's favorites: her famous Chocolate pancakes, bacon, eggs and cheese grits. She thought he would sit and talk to her for a minute since they never got a chance to see each other. But, he got his plate and went into his office. She sat in the kitchen for a minute before she started to flip through her cookbooks, looking for ideas about what to prepare for the week's meals. She checked the freezer and found left over meatloaf and tuna casserole. She decided to bake two chickens and make a pot roast. Both would be quick, and she could cook the vegetables at the same time.

Sherese set about her tasks, made lunches and put them in the brown paper bags. She drew smiley faces and put extra treats in each one. It was almost noon, and she was mopping the kitchen floor when the phone rang. She went to answer it but Steve already had it. When she answered, there was silence. She dialed *69 again. It was an unknown number. The phone rang again and this time, and it was her mother.

"Sherese, you don't go to Macy's on Fridays do you?"

"No, mom, I don't. Why do you ask?"

"Baby, I need to talk to you. Can you come over after work then?"

"Are you okay, do you need something?"

"Yes, I'm okay. I don't need anything, other than to talk to you."

"Well mom, we can talk anytime."

"No, I want to talk to you on Friday, before the kids need to be picked up from school. I will expect you by 3:15."

"But mom, you know I do all my grocery shopping on Friday's after work and pick up the dry cleaning and get little things the kids need."

"BE HERE BY 3:15 on FRIDAY."

Sherese started to object, but knew better. She held the phone for a minute, wondering what that was about. *I've told Autumn not to play in her grannies things. She probably used up all moms' expensive perfume again. I'll get her a new bottle when I go to work tonight. They are having a one-day sale and with my discount I can probably afford it.*

Sherese finished mopping the floor, and still had four hours before she had to go in to work. She went into Steve's office where he was working on the computer. She tiptoed up behind him and started to nibble on his ear.

He turned to look at her. "Sherese, you smell like onions. What were you cooking?"

Sherese ignored him and continued to nibble on his ear. "Come take a shower with me. I've been a very naughty girl. I need to be punished with that big magic stick of yours."

Steve smiled, as he grabbed her face in his hands and kissed her. "Honey, that sounds so tempting, but I have so many pages that I have to get out today. I've found an agent in New York and he wants to look at some of my work. I sent him a query letter and he asked that I send him fifty pages. So, I need to get to work and make sure everything is all polished and looking good. This could be the break I've been looking for. I could sell one of my books, get my name out there, and it will be a best seller I know it will! Then, you can quit your jobs and we could travel all over the world."

Sherese smiled at the idea. She began to embroider his dream, adding, "Then you could be on Good Morning America and the Tonight show. They'll want to make the book into a movie and Entertainment Tonight will want to do interviews about our family. We'll be invited to the best parties and the kids can have the best private school educations." The thought of it all made her ecstatic. She smiled and kissed her husband again. "Well, go ahead and make it happen, baby. I'm behind you all the way. But if you need to take a break, I'll be upstairs trying not to be a naughty girl."

Steve patted her rear as she walked away. Sherese went upstairs, wondering what to do with herself. She cleaned out the clothes hamper and started to do laundry. As the clothes were washing she decided to take a bubble bath. She hoped Steve would be tempted to come join her. She heard the buzzer on the dryer go off and noticed the clock. She had just enough time to put the last load in, fold the clothes and get to work.

After work, she picked up the kids. Her mom had them ready. She tried to talk to her mom so she could avoid spending Friday afternoon with her. She had so much to do, but Maime didn't budge.

"I'll see *you* on Friday."

Sherese was dreading Friday. She could tell from her mother's tone that she was upset about something. She asked the kids if they had been bad and of course, they said, "No mommy, we've been very good like you told us."

When Sherese arrived for work on Friday, there was a note on her desk for her to see Tom when she got in. She knocked on his office door.

"Come in and close the door behind you."

She sat down, wondering what the office gossip was. Tom and Sherese always traded stories about what was going on with their coworkers, but, for some reason, Tom was not his jovial self. He couldn't quite look her in the eye.

"What's going on, Tom?"

"Sherese, you and I have been friends for a long time and when I got promoted, I fought to bring you with me. Each step I've made in the company, we've made together, but this is no longer working out. You've been late three days this week and it was only a four-day workweek. You've been missing deadlines, coming to work improperly groomed and acting like you're drugged. Mike wants me to fire you, but I stuck my neck on the line to protect you because we have been friends and you have been so valuable to me in the past."

Sherese shook her head from side to side, wondering whether she was really hearing the words coming out of Tom's mouth.

"Sherese, I won't continue to put my job on the line to protect you. I have a note on my house, my timeshare in Vail-- not to mention the payment for my new jag. I like you, Sherese, but you have to start pulling your weight around here. You are going to be placed on a ninety-day probation starting today and your work will be monitored by Mike and myself. He's looking for a reason to fire you and he's given very valid reasons about why he thinks that firing you is the appropriate thing to do. Look at you. Your clothes are rough dried and that ponytail has been in your hair for weeks now. Your nail polish is chipped and Mike doesn't want the clients seeing you look like this. This is not the secretary pool. This is the corporate executive floor. I keep telling Mike that you used to be the best, that you are having some personal problems that you've trying to work out, and that I'm trying to help you. He said to fire you, lay you off and give you the option for re-hire in six months, or let you take a leave of absence without pay to get your situation straightened out. I told him I felt I owed you a chance and that's why I suggested a probation period. Mike was adamant; he said something had to be done. He understands how good you used to be, but he says, 'Used-to-bees don't make no honey.'"

Sherese sat stunned; she couldn't believe this was happening. She couldn't believe Tom would betray her like this. Sherese looked at Tom with tears in her eyes.

"How could you? After all the times I've covered your butt and worked extra for you over the last seven years?"

"Don't you dare raise your voice at me! Our past is exactly why security is not escorting you to your car as we speak. But if that is what you want, I can arrange that."

"You know I can't afford to lose my job."

"Then you need to work like you don't want to lose your job. You sent the wrong report to Mr. Wilson. The month end report had all the wrong data and you were four days late on the oil runs. To make matters worse you used an old pricing chart to distribute costs to the joint venture partners. That error cost us over $60,000. Plus, you come in almost everyday looking like shit. Anybody else would have been gone! You cannot expect to work three jobs, take care of two kids and a household, and not let something slip. Now, here's what I propose. You have six days in comp time and three weeks of vacation. Take it and come back ready to work your ass off."

"I can't. It won't be much longer. My husband finally found a literary agent in New York and he is on the verge of selling his book. I need the vacation and comp time to be with the children when they are off at Christmas break."

"Sherese, something has to give. When are you going to wake up and smell the coffee? Steve has not worked in almost four years. Hell, you could write a whole encyclopedia in four years. Every couple of months, he thinks he has a new agent. I feel for you, but I will not put myself in jeopardy any longer. Mike is watching how I handle this situation. Since you don't want to take the vacation, take the comp time, plan what you want to do or look for another job."

"I'll quit the morning job," she bargained. "That should help me get to work on time and I'll tell Steve that he is going to have to do something to help me. But, I hate to! I know you don't believe it. But, he is so close this time."

"Of course he is," Tom said, looking at Sherese with a smirk on his face.

Sherese could tell that he was patronizing her.

Sherese began to cry. "I'll work things out somehow. You won't be sorry, Tom."

Tom gave her hand a squeeze, "Take the rest of the day off. Today's time will not come out of your comp time, and I padded your numbers so it's okay."

Sherese could only nod, yes. Her eyes were too full of tears to speak.

She wondered if she could convince Steve to get a part-time job for a few hours a day or maybe a weekend job, so they could manage. But the last time they had that discussion, Steve said he wasn't going to work on any penny-ante job that didn't appreciate him or pay him what he was worth. He said he wasn't going to take any ole job.

Sherese thought, *I'll explain that the economy is not doing that well and that he shouldn't expect to make what he was making before he was laid off. I'll have to let him know that times are very hard. Maybe we should sell the house and get something smaller.*

But they didn't really have that much equity in the house. They had lived there less than six months before Steve was laid off. Maybe she could talk to Larry, Steve's old boss, to see if the company could call Steve back to work. Her mind was a whirlwind. She knew that if she lost her job, everything would fall apart. Maybe she could ask her mother for some help--or her father. Lord knows he hadn't done anything in the past.

Maybe he could help out now. Or maybe Steve could ask his mother.

Sherese braced herself for more bad news as she arrived at her mom's house a little early and found her making BLT's and cinnamon tea. Sherese got the plates from the cabinet and sat opposite her mom, trying to discern what this little talk of hers was all about. Her mom placed Sherese's favorite lemon icebox pie on the table and took a long look at her daughter.

Her mom finally spoke. "There is nothing in heaven or earth that I love more than you. I'd give my life for you or either one of my grandchildren."

Sherese attempted to interrupt, but her mother silenced her and continued. "I raised you the best way I knew how and gave you all the things you needed and most of the things you wanted because I thought that was a mother's duty."

Sherese interrupted, "But you are a great mom . . ."

Maime ignored Sherese and kept talking. "But now, I have to draw the line. I'm fifty-six years-old and I hope I have some good years left in me. I retired to try to get some living done ... living I could not do when you were a child because I had to take care of you and make sure that you were strong, healthy and happy. Now, I'm planning to get back some of the living I lost. Sherese, I love you but Autumn and Anthony are your children. You need to raise them and be their mother. My life is tied up with them every evening and most weekends. There are things that I want to do that I can't do because I have to be home with your children. That is not a grandmother's role. It's your role. I've been thinking about this for a long time. Sherese, you're going to have to take your children back. Do you have any idea what is going on in their lives? Who their friends are? What class projects they have to complete?"

Sherese tried to speak, but her mom continued.

"Last week, Autumn took $50 from my purse. I missed it when I went to the pharmacy to get my prescription. I knew it was there the night before because I broke a hundred dollar bill to buy pizza for them. When I picked them up from school, I asked them both about it and Anthony confessed that Autumn had taken it. She wanted to buy James, a boy in her class that she likes, a Steve Madden Video game."

Sherese gasped for air and sat with her mouth ajar. She couldn't believe it. Autumn was only ten years old. Maime noticed her reaction but kept talking.

"I talked to her and asked her why she did it and she said that she wanted him to like her. I told her that buying expensive gifts was not the way to get someone to like you. Then Autumn looked at me defiantly and said, 'That's what mommy does for daddy.'"

Sherese's jaw dropped and she started to speak, but her mom interrupted.

"Wait, I'm not finished. I told Autumn that she was going to have to work to pay back the money. I made a little chart for each thing she does and I subtract it from the total she owes."

Maime got up, put the chart in front of her shocked daughter, and continued.

"She gets $2.00 for raking leaves, $1.00 for dishes, $1.00 for dusting, $1.00 for making sure all of her and her brother's clothes are put in the hamper and so forth."

Sherese opened her purse. "Mom I'll give you the money back."

Maime gave her a stern look. "That is not the issue Sherese. Have you being listening to me? I thought we were both speaking English."

Sherese was quiet, waiting for her mother to get to the issue.

"The issue is that your daughter thinks she can buy some kid's affection and that she has gotten this idea from you. When I think about it, you had to get it from me. When I think about it, that is all you know because you saw me take up all the slack for your father. I really loved him, as I know you really love Steve, but your father was not a good man and neither is Steve. It is too late for me to make wrong things right, but it is not too late for you."

She continued, "I thought I was doing the right thing because I wanted to keep my family together, but your father was a gambler. He always worked but, sometimes, before he got home, his paycheck was gone. I started going to his job and getting his paycheck directly from his boss. That worked for a while, but he became resentful and began pawning everything that he could get his hands on so he could have money to gamble with his hoodlum friends. His gambling got so bad that he was fired from his jobs because he had bookies and bad men coming to his job to beat him up for not paying his gambling debts. It got so bad that I had to close every bank account we had and sleep with every dollar we had pinned inside my bra. I know now that I should have left him to protect you from seeing him that way. But, I stayed and you saw me handling everything by myself and since that is all you saw, you began to think that was the way life was supposed to be. I apologize, Sherese, I didn't know I was harming you. In my heart, I thought I was doing the right thing, but as I see Autumn, I know that this vicious cycle has to stop here. I need you to take the lead. You're working yourself to death, and I'm watching you age before my eyes. I pray every day that you won't fall asleep at the wheel or get robed leaving the mall at night or get carjacked out 5 am while throwing newspapers. I'm scared for you, Sherese. I know you love your husband, and you should. But, love is about sharing and taking care of each other. Steve is a selfish child who has found two new mothers--you and me."

Sherese was getting angry. *How can she say that my husband doesn't love me?*

"Mom, you have no idea how much Steve loves me. It hurts him to see me work the way I do, but he knows that it will be all better when his book is published. He is very close. He has this new agent in New York . . ."

Maime interrupted. "Sherese, if Steve loved you, he'd help you. If it hurt him to see you work three jobs, he'd get at least one. Most people don't have the luxury to quit their jobs to work on books that no one ever gets to read. When is the last time you read anything he wrote?"

Sherese couldn't remember. He'd stopped letting her read anything once she told him that an article he wrote needed a little more work. He'd accused her of not supporting him. Out of all the books she'd read, Steve's book was the worst. The stories were hard to follow, they lacked character development, the grammar wasn't good and if she had been honest, she would have told him so years ago, but she didn't want to discourage him from following his dreams. He believed that a reader had to be an intellect to appreciate his books.

"Mom, Steve loves me, but it makes him nervous when I read his stories."

"I have been seeing a therapist over the last six months and I've discovered a lot of things. I think we should all go as a family," Maime said.

"Do I need a therapist, just because I love and support my husband?" asked Sherese.

"No," Maime said, shaking her head. "You need a therapist because you came from a dysfunctional family and you're creating a dysfunctional family of your very own." Maime paused, "I started seeing a therapist after your father wrote me a letter telling me that I had saved his life by leaving him. He finally sought help in a twelve-step program."

Handing the letter to her daughter, she continued through tears.

"Your father said, with me by his side, he was able to gamble and he wanted to thank me for leaving him. I decided to go to a therapist because I realized that he was right. Through therapy I discovered I am what they call an enabler. There is a condition that describes how I have lived my life. It's called Co-Dependent. I was co-dependent with him and co-dependent with you and you're co-dependent with Steve. Sherese, it has to stop somewhere. It's a mother's duty to make hard decisions, so that's what I'm doing. I will no longer enable you. If you chose to enable Steve, then that is your own business. What I would like is for you to come with me to see my therapist. If you decide to go, that would make me very happy. If not, I'll release you to find your own way. But, you're going to have to find someone to pick up the children from school and care for them until you get off work. I'll continue for the next two weeks, but after that, I'm taking a trip. Cousin Estella and I are going to nine countries in Europe. We will be gone for six weeks. My child is grown and I can afford it, so I'm doing it. After I get back, I'm finally going to take that ballroom dancing class I always wanted to take and I'm also thinking about taking a computer class at the community college. Whatever is left of my life, I'm planning on living it. I hope you'll find a way to live yours, Sherese. It's easier at thirty-two than fifty-six."

Maime pulled out the brochures and showed her daughter all the exotic places she was going to visit. She was so proud to show off her brand new passport. Sherese was happy for her mom, but wondered how she would manage. First, Tom, now, her mom. No one understood what she was going through. She knew Steve loved her and would come through. She wanted to feel sorry for herself, but she didn't have time. She had thirty minutes to get cross-town to pick up Anthony and Autumn.

Her children were glad to see here. They asked about granny and why she didn't pick them up. Sherese said, "I wanted to pick you up because I love you and couldn't wait to see you."

She gave them a rare treat and took them to McDonald's. She asked about school as they ate and they bombarded her with tales about classmates, teachers and friends. She even let them play in the balls until they wore themselves out. They eyed her suspiciously as they went up and down the little castle ladders into the huge vat of balls. Sherese's mind was going a mile a minute. How would she manage? How would she tell Steve? He was so close this time, she didn't want to set him back, but there was no choice. She could probably find a transportation company to pick them up from the after school program by 6:00 pm and drop them at home. But, that would cost money she didn't have. She was already quitting the morning job. She couldn't afford to quit the evening job. She knew she was going to have to keep the day job or find a new day job that paid enough to make up the difference between the other two. But she didn't know what kind of references she would get.

Sherese called her boss and told him that something had come up and she'd changed her mind about taking a week in comp time. Tom agreed, it was a good decision. She called her mom and asked if she would do her one more big favor, and take the kids on Sunday, because she wanted to talk things over with Steve. Her mom agreed and wished her luck.

The kids went to sleep in the car. All of that hollering and running back and forth had worn them completely out. Sherese went inside to get Steve to help her carry them upstairs, but the door to his office was closed and he was typing away. Sherese carried the children upstairs one at a time, put them to bed after she kissed them good night; she unloaded the groceries in the trunk. She decided to do her weekly cooking, since the kids were asleep and Steve's office door was closed.

With all the cooking done, she went back to Steve's office. He was reading over some papers. He looked up, saw her and asked her to bring him a piece of pie and a glass of milk. She brought his goodies and then asked when he was coming to bed. With an irritated look on his face, he retorted, "Sherese, I'm trying to concentrate."

Sherese excused herself and closed the door behind her.

It was close to midnight and she had to be up early. She wanted to try to wait for Steve, but it wasn't long before sleep took over.

When the alarm clock went off, she checked it by the VCR clock because she was sure she had just gone to bed. She got up, got dressed and drove her route with relative ease before heading to Macy's. Most of the day was a blur because her mind was elsewhere. She managed to smile at complaining customers and co-workers. She'd worked at Macy's since high school and was what they called permanent part-time. Since she worked thirty hours a week, she got most of the benefits that the full-time staff got. She checked and she had almost three weeks vacation. That would buy her some time until Steve found a job. She knew things would work out some way.

Sherese got home at 6:00 pm. It was still light, so she decided to take Autumn and Anthony to the movies to see Spy Kids. They were ecstatic: she had a lot of making up to do and she wanted to start with them right away. Watching them, she realized that she had missed so much of their lives. After the movie, she took the kids home, fed them dinner and told them to go up and take their baths while she washed and ironed their clothes for the week and started making lunches.

She wrote her letter of resignation for the morning job. Since she had decided to take the week of comp time, she gave them a week to replace her. Then, she sat down with the family finances and paid the bills for the month. With all three jobs, she was barely making ends meet. All the credit cards were maxed out. For a year, the credit cards had been her saving grace, but, now, she could barely keep up with the minimum payments. She couldn't even afford to get her dry cleaning out. Some miracle would have to happen. She fantasized about Steve getting a $50,000 advance for his book. They could pay off both cars and the credit cards. She relished in the idea for a minute, before coming back to reality. If push came to shove, she thought she could add Friday evening to her Macys schedule and work six hours on Sunday from 12:00-6:00 pm. That would give her forty hours a week plus two hours overtime. It wouldn't be hard to do because someone was always calling in or wanting someone to work for them on the weekend. If she did that, she could almost make up for the lost income from the morning job.

She carefully looked over the budget for things to cut out. There was nothing other than food, and that wasn't much. She was the queen of grocery coupons. She rarely bought anything to wear; thank God she always stayed the same size. She bought all the kids clothes when Macy's had sales and with the extra value coupons and her employee discount, she did pretty well. Sherese decided to discuss it with Steve; it was too much for her to handle by herself. She walked by his office before going to bed. He was whispering in the phone. *Probably his crazy mama,* she thought.

Sherese got up early Sunday morning and ran her route. She gave her notice. Her supervisor was sorry to see her go. He said she was the most dependable driver he had. Instead of listening to the radio, which usually kept her company, Sherese drove her route in silence. She prayed, asking God for a miracle. When she finished her route, she went home and dressed the kids for church with their Granny. They loved Sunday School, which was strange because she had always hated it. She fixed each child's favorites for breakfast and took them to her mother's house. Her mom kissed each one of the children and gave her daughter a big hug.

When she returned home, Steve was still sleeping. She took off all her clothes and looked at herself in the mirror. She was still an attractive woman. She had to admit she did look older than her years, but her body was still firm and slender. She'd gotten good 'slim genes' from her mother and father. She had only gained a little over thirty pounds during her pregnancies, so it had been easy getting back down to her normal size.

Now, she took a long bath, put on her best nightgown, made her face up and put on her favorite cologne. After all the preparations, Steve was still sleeping, so she went downstairs and brought up a breakfast tray for him. She woke him with breakfast in bed. He devoured every last morsel, but didn't notice that she was wearing the nightgown from their honeymoon.

When he said he was going to go play golf with the fellows, Sherese told him, "Steve, I need to talk to you."

"Let's talk later, I don't want to be late."

"No, Steve it can't wait."

Irritated, and not trying to hide it, he sat down on the bed, annoyed at her insistence. Sherese told him about her conversation with Tom, her conversation with her mother and about their family finances.

When she finished, Steve said, "I told you years ago that Tom was a damn snake in the grass and, I hate to say it, but your mom is one selfish woman. How in the hell does she think we are going to survive?"

Sherese resisted telling him that *his* mother had never done anything to help them and the dollar store toys she bought the kids at Christmas were ridiculous. But, she didn't want to start that argument.

"Steve, I need some help. I can't do it alone. You're going to have to get a job and help out more with the kids," Sherese said, in a pleading voice.

Steve got up angrily, and said, "I knew you were going to start some shit. Every time I get on a roll with my work, you come out of the blue and start some damn shit. I can't handle it this morning. My mother warned me about you and I should have listened."

Still trying to keep the peace, Sherese said, "Baby, I'm not trying to start anything. This family has some problems and all I'm asking you is to try and give me some help."

"Help my ass," Steve bellowed. "You're a fucking albatross around my neck!"

Through tears, Sherese said, "Steve, I can't do it alone anymore. I need you. Don't walk away from me. We have $378 in the bank--that's all we have, Steve."

"Then you need to stop fucking off the money. What happened to the savings we had?"

"In case you haven't noticed, we have bills to pay, a house note, utilities, two car notes, furniture, your damn golf club membership and two kids who have to be clothed and fed. How do you think those things get paid, Steve? The last time you worked or brought a dollar into this house was three years and eleven months ago."

"I knew it wouldn't be long before you were throwing that shit up in my face. What about all the years I worked?"

"I worked those years, too, Steve. The only time I haven't worked two jobs was when I was on maternity leave and even then I still got paid. How can you say you love me when I work three jobs and you don't even have a part-time job? I'm not asking you to give up your dream, I'm just asking that you help me with our kids and the bills we have to pay."

"I'm not listening to this shit, fuck you, Sherese."

"While we're on the subject of fucking me," Sherese said, "Why haven't you in over six months? Why is it that you're always too busy for me? You used to love to make love to me."

"You're damned right, used to."

Steve's words stabbed Sherese. She didn't know what to say, and it wouldn't have mattered because he was out of the door and down the steps.

Sherese cried herself to sleep. She woke with swollen eyes and smeared make-up, her head and stomach were aching. It was almost 7 o'clock. Steve hadn't come home yet, so she showered and drove to her mother's to pick up the children. Maime took one look at her and knew that it had not gone well with Steve. But, she didn't say a word. She asked if she wanted some dinner.

Sherese refused and rounded up the children and headed for home. She expected to see Steve's car when she opened the garage, but his space was empty. Sherese put the kids to bed and finished making their lunches. She tried to watch television until Steve got in, but fell into a fretful sleep. When she woke to do her route, the kids were sleeping, so she left them alone and went to do her job. When she returned, they were still sleeping. By the time she got them up, they had missed the bus, so she drove them to school. When she called Lynsey, she agreed to meet her for breakfast.

Lynsey listened as her friend poured out her heart between gasps for air and nose blowing. Lynsey didn't offer any advice. She'd been there too many times before; she knew the drill, and Sherese would be back in love with Steve within minutes.

Lynsey listened and shook her head. Lynsey had called in and said she was going to be late, but she didn't want to be too late. She hugged Sherese goodbye and headed to work.

Sherese headed home. When she opened the garage, she was relieved to see Steve's car, but shocked to see a blue Toyota Camry parked next to it. She was even more shocked to see a woman, wearing nothing but Sherese's apron, standing in the kitchen with Steve pressed against her. They didn't hear Sherese come in; they had the music playing loud and were heavily engaged in foreplay. Sherese grabbed a large pepper shaker from the counter.

Steve turned around, surprised, and said, "Oh, hello Sherese. I wanted you to see who I enjoy fucking now."

The girl looked young. She didn't say a word. She just grinned at Sherese. Sherese screamed at her to get out of her damned house. The woman didn't move.

"Go ahead and go, I have some business to attend to, I'll be over shortly," Steve said.

She didn't bother to put any clothes on; she left with Sherese's apron, picking up her clothes on the way out.

Steve turned to Sherese, who was still holding the pepper shaker. He said, "You see, Sherese, I don't have to take your shit. I have plenty of women who would love to support me."

"How could you do this to me after all I've done for you and this family?

"It was hard to stomach living with you. You owed me for just being with you."

"Get out of here you bastard," Sherese screamed.

Steve grabbed her and slung her over the table. He tore her t-shirt off of her and held her down as he pulled down her sweat pants and had his way with her.

Over and over again, he yelled, "Is that what you want Sherese?" She couldn't believe her own body as it began to move beneath him and betray her good senses. Sherese shuddered from tears as a huge orgasm hit her at the same time. Steve smiled and walked to his office, got his computer and walked out.

After sitting on the cold tile floor with her sweat pants around one ankle, she made her way to her feet. She stood there for a couple of minutes trying to find her bearings. She walked to the phone, her pants still around her ankle. She took the phone book out, called a locksmith and her mom. She asked her mom to pick up the kids and keep them for the night. She said she'd explain later. Maime could tell she had been crying, and it took all she had not to run to her child and try to make it all right. Sherese finally pulled her pants up and took a clean t-shirt out of the dryer.

She went to the garage, changed the code on the garage door opener. Her next call was to Brinks to change the security code and the emergency password. Next, she called a friend from Macy's who was looking for extra hours and agreed to work for Sherese all week. The next phone call was to a divorce attorney. The next was to a real estate broker.

With each phone call, Sherese got a little stronger. She felt the life force returning to her body. Sherese knew she would be all right. When the time came, she had known exactly what to do. Her mom kept the kids, while she packed all of Steve's possessions, and got her house ready for the realtor to show.

She stopped to read some papers he had left where the computer had been. She laughed and said, "It will be a cold day in hell before this is ever published." She packed his office, then rented a van to take all of his belongings to his mother's house.

Steve tried to contest the divorce, but he couldn't afford a lawyer. When the judge saw proof that Steve had not paid a dime into the household for four years, Sherese was granted the house, all furnishings and—yes, the bills too. Steve would have to find a job to pay the court awarded $700.00 a month in child support. When she sold the house, she didn't make anything off the sale, but her mother let her borrow enough money for a down payment on a smaller house that she could afford. As Sherese walked out of the courtroom and thanked her lawyer for all her help, she began to feel a little queasy. She made it to the bathroom just in time to throw up, an awful tasting yellow bile that filled her stomach. The only time she had ever had that experience was when she was pregnant. She sat on the toilet. Could it be? She couldn't think of the last time she'd had a period.

1.   Sherese should
      A.   Go back to her husband for the sake of her children.
      B.   Make Steve pay through the nose.
      C.   Cut her losses and move on.
2.   Sherese should realize
      A.   Men cheat, and cheating is not grounds for leaving a marriage.
      B.   Revenge is best served cold.
      C.   That if he cheats once he will do it again.
3.   Sherese should
      A.   Put her children's needs above her own.
      B.   Use her children to create havoc in Steve's life.
      C.   Create a better example for her children.
4.   Sherese should
      A.   Decide to have the baby and reconcile with Steve.
      B.   Have the baby and get more child support.
      C.   Abort the baby so she can afford to take care of the two children she already has.
5.   Sherese should
      A.   Try to put the past behind her, especially since her children are small.
      B.   Find a way to make Steve pay.
      C.   Concentrate on trying to raise her kids by herself.
6.   Sherese needs to know that
      A.   Single parent families are unstable.
      B.   Steve is unstable.

C. Single mothers can effectively raise children.

7. Sherese should tell her children
  A. That grown-ups sometimes have arguments and assure them that it is not their fault.
  B. Their father left them for another woman.
  C. That both their parents love them, but they can't all live together any more.

8. Sherese should
  A. Seek counseling for her children.
  B. Make sure everyone knows Steve is a deadbeat dad.
  C. Find ways to take care of her children without Steve.

9. Sherese's goal should be
  A. Reconciliation with her husband.
  B. To get the maximum amount of child support from Steve.
  C. To make a parenting plan with Steve.

10. Sherese should
  A. Put her children's happiness above her own.
  B. Make Steve's life miserable.
  C. Realize her needs are important for a healthy family.

11. Sherese has to
  A. Take Steve back if she expects to make it.
  B. Make sure Steve is so broke that no one will want him.
  C. Find additional sources of income.

If your answers total
> Mostly A's read ending X
> Mostly B's read ending Y
> Mostly C's read ending Z

Ending X

"Miss, will that be all for you?"

"Miss!" the woman repeated.

"Yes, that will be it," Sherese said, shaking off the haze. It took a second for her to remember where she was. She swiped her credit card, took the small bag and headed for the door, but decided she couldn't wait to get home. She needed to know now, if she was pregnant. The Value Mart bathroom was a mess; water, paper towels and toilet paper were all over the floor. There were several unflushed toilets that were probably the source of the stench. Sherese almost turned around at the sight and smell, but decided her life was a mess so it was a fitting place for her to find out just how big of a mess it was.

Sherese prayed, one of those, "I'll do anything if . . . prayers," before she tore into the home pregnancy package. She was supposed to wait two minutes to see if the plus sign showed in the little window, but it seemed to only take seconds before the plus sign was visible. Sherese sat for a long time staring at the floor with all of its embedded dirt and grime. Her cell phone ring brought her back to reality. She was late to pick up the kids from school.

Sherese drove frantically, weaving from lane to lane, trying to make it to the school before the principal called the authorities. She'd been late three times this week and it was only

Wednesday. Sherese popped a wheelie into the parking lot to see three sets of legs sitting on the curb. She thought she was seeing things when she saw Steve's wide grin smiling at her as she approached the kids.

"What are you doing here, Steve?" Sherese said, jumping out of the car and hugging her kids.

"I just wanted to see them. I tried to call you to tell I'd pick them up, but you didn't answer the phone. . . "

"Mommy! Mommy! Daddy is going to take us for pizza, Anthony said, pulling on her jacket pocket.

"Oh, honey that's great."

"If that's all right with you, Sherese. I tried to call you to clear it with you . . ."

"That's fine. You have a good time. Give mommy a kiss," Sherese said, smiling at her son.

"Sherese, why don't you come with us, you used to love Mr. Gattis' pizza."

"Please mommy, please," the kids shouted in unison.

"No, you all have a good time. I've got plenty of work to do. I'll see you two later," Sherese said, kissing the tops of their heads. "Okay, if you're sure you can't eat one slice of pizza."

"I'm sure."

"Sherese, why don't I keep them tonight and take them to school in the morning? They have clothes at my house," said Steve

"Please mommy! Can we?" the kids pleaded.

"Sure, it's all right with me. But make sure they do their homework and Anthony has his breathing treatment before bed. Here, I have an extra inhaler in my bag."

The Pregnancy Test fell from her purse as she reached for the inhaler.

"What is this, Sherese?" asked Steve.

"What does it look like?"

"Kids, go and sit in daddy's car. I have to talk to mommy for a minute," said Steve.

"Well, what were the results and who's the father?" Steve demanded, holding the package in his hands.

"I don't want to talk about this now."

"Dammit, Sherese, you couldn't even wait for the ink was dry on the divorce papers before you went and got yourself knocked up, by God knows who."

"Lower your voice and for your information, I didn't get knocked up. My husband raped me in my own damned kitchen." Sherese watched as the blood drained from Steve's face. He looked as if he was going to faint.

"Get your damned hands off me," Sherese shouted as Steve tried to touch her arm.

Sherese got in her car and sped out of the parking lot and in to oncoming traffic, coming within a fraction on an inch from hitting a red Honda.

At home, she sat in her driveway in a daze, contemplating how she got home and how she'd manage.

What am I going to do? I can't have another baby. I can barely afford the two I already have. I can't start over with a newborn . . . sleepless *nights, diapers and $150 a week child care. What am I going to do? I'm hanging on to my job by a string and I'm going on four months pregnant. What am I going to do? I can't keep this baby. With the company going through a merger, I can't take maternity leave. They'd lay me off for sure. I'm still on probation and I know Tom is watching my every move."*

Sherese was pulled out of her daze by Steve's tapping on the window.

"Sherese, we've got to talk about this."

"Go away, Steve. Leave me alone!" Sherese shouted through the closed window.

"Get out of the car, Sherese, we need to talk."

"No, go away please."

Steve used his key and opened the car door. Sherese was stunned. She didn't even think to ask for her keys back. He reached in and hugged her.

Stroking her hair he said, "Come on baby, let's go inside."

"Where are the kids, Steve?"

"They're at your mother's. I told her the news."

"You did what?" Sherese shouted, pulling free of his embrace. "You don't have any right to tell my business."

"Our business, Sherese, let's go inside."

"Sherese, you know I love you. These last months without you have been hard."

"I'm sure they have been. You've had to pay your own damned bills."

"I deserve that. I know I lost myself for awhile, but I'm back on track now. I have a job now and I know we can make this thing work. I miss you, Sherese and I miss seeing my kids everyday."

"You didn't miss them for all the years we were together, you never did anything with them and you brought that damn tramp into our house, Steve. And you raped me!"

"Sherese, let's put the past behind us. I'm a new man now and I want my family back and our unborn child. I got lost for a minute baby, but I'm back. I've been talking to the Pastor and he helped me see that, the problem was not you. I was supposed to be the man of the house. I know it's going to be tough, but we can make it. I promise. Will you TRUST ME? I'll make it up to you. Baby, please give me a chance."

Sherese melted into Steve's arms. Steve became the husband Sherese had always wanted: attentive, loving and thoughtful. He helped the kids with homework, did dishes and even cooked once or twice a week. Their life was bliss.

Five months later Sherese went into labor. At the hospital, the doctor looked frantic when her daughter emerged from her mother's womb, and even the nurse stood with her mouth agape. Someone shoved surgery consent papers at Sherese and Steve as the doctor shouted commands to the staff. A second doctor rushed in and took the baby's tiny body to surgery. Sherese pleaded with the nurse to tell her what was wrong with her baby. After what seemed like days, the doctor came in to explain that the baby was a Gastroskesis baby, born with her intestines outside of her body. She had required immediate surgery and would need lots of special care. Steve held Sherese close and tried to dry her tears even though he couldn't stop his own.

They named the baby Aaralyn, which meant 'with song.' It seemed to describe their life together the second time around.

Aaralyn came home from the hospital after six weeks and two surgeries. The medical costs were mounting and the song that had described their life began to sound like a scratched record. Steve and Sherese decided to hire a live-in nanny to take care of Aaralyn, get the kids to and from school, cook and do minor housework. They both worked long hours to make ends meet. After all the turmoil, it seemed like they were finding their rhythm again.

For months they were a team, but it didn't last long. The hang-ups started. Steve started to work late a lot. Sherese became suspicious when the overtime pay didn't show up in his paycheck. It didn't take long to sniff out the truth. She decided to call his job.

"Hello, Manny, this is Sherese, Steve's wife. If he's not too busy can I speak to him?'

" . . . Sherese, Steve doesn't work here anymore. Friday was his last day. He resigned."

"What? When did this happen?"

"He gave us thirty days notice. We even offered him a raise for him to stay, but he said he was going to work on his writing full-time."

"Thanks, Manny I appreciate all your help," Sherese said after a long pause.

"I'm sorry. You mean to tell me, you didn't know he was quitting?"

"No, Manny. I didn't know."

"Well, tell him he can come back anytime. We really hated to lose him."

"Okay, Manny, I'll make sure he knows.

Sherese drove to the apartment complex of the woman who Steve had brought to her house the day that Aaralyn was conceived. Sherese remembered her tag number and got her address from the policeman who worked as security guard at her building. She had known this information would come in handy one day. Sherese waited for almost thirty minutes until she could follow someone through the security gates, and almost rear-ended the car in front of her. It didn't take long to spot Steve's car parked haphazardly next to the blue Toyota she had seen in her garage that day.

"Excuse me, Miss," Sherese said to the young woman taking out her trash. "I just nicked the paint on this car and I want to tell the owner, do you know who this car belongs to?"

"Wow, that is so honest of you. Someone backed into my car and totally left the scene and didn't even leave a note. I was so mad."

"Well, I know what you mean. That's why I want to let them know.'

"I'm sure she'll be glad you did. I don't know her name but she lives upstairs, the first apartment to the left, where the wreath is on the door."

"Thank you."

"No, Thank you for being so honest. I wish more people were like you."

Sherese nodded, walked up the stairs, and was about to knock on the door when the woman who had been wearing her apron, opened the door to exit. Sherese pushed her back inside.

"What the hell are you doing, Steve?" shouted Sherese

"Get the hell out of my house, who do you think you are pushing your way in here like the police," said the apron-wearing woman.

"Steve, what the hell are you doing? Manny said you quit your job."

"Sherese, it's too much for me. Three kids, one of them sick, and all the medical bills. I need my freedom. You all are sucking the life out of me. I don't love you anymore."

"That's right bitch, he doesn't love you! Now get out of my house," said his angry girlfriend.

Sherese turned on her heels and headed for the door. She felt the wind from the ashtray thrown in her direction, right before she turned and knocked Steve's girlfriend to the floor in a single blow.

The second divorce was quick. Steve was ordered to get a job and pay $1,200.00 a month in child support or go to jail. Sherese hugged her kids when she got home and reassured them that their daddy loved them. She didn't know how, but she knew they'd make it.

Ending Y

The idea that she could be pregnant made Sherese's blood boil.

"He thinks he can just walk away and leave me holding the bag with three children and one I didn't even ask for. He thinks he can cough up $700 a month and that's it. Well, he has another thought coming." Sherese was thinking out loud. The woman in the courthouse bathroom stall next to her wondered what was going on. Sherese pulled out her cell phone and called her attorney.

"Melanie, this is Sherese. I think I'm pregnant. Can we take Steve back to court?"

"Well, Yes, but you'll have to know for sure and we'll have to prove paternity."

"That won't be a problem. I'm going to make an appointment to verify my suspicions. I'll call you with the results."

Sherese left the doctor's office with a sinister smile on her face.

"Steve, I just called to congratulate you. You're going to be a dad again. Thanks to that little stint in the kitchen about four months ago."

"What are you talking about?"

"You know damn well what I'm talking about. You raped me. You're going to pay. Wow, I get a chance to smother your ass with child support payments. With a newborn, the expenses go up, up, up and for the next eighteen years I'll make you suffer."

"If your dumb ass is pregnant, you better find someone else to pin it on."

"Oh, but the DNA test will show who the father is and then you will Show me the Money."

Steve sat holding the phone, wishing he were close enough to Sherese to shove it down her throat. He knew he'd never survive if he had to pay child support for three children. He'd talked his mother into paying the $700 a month for a year until his book was finished.

Ariel was born on her father's birthday. What a coincidence Sherese thought. She was tested and the results came back 99.89% that Steve was the child's biological father. Sherese held Ariel proudly as the court docket was called. Steven was a no-show to the proceedings. The judge increased the child support to $1280.00 per month. But Steve didn't care. He'd borrowed $5,000 from his mother, packed up his car, changed his name, bought a fake social security number and moved to Los Angeles to look for an agent for his book and the screenplay he wanted to write about his life. Sherese didn't get a dime in child support to help her take care of her three children.

Ending Z

"Melanie, this is Sherese. I have a quick question for you concerning my divorce."

"Okay, Shoot. I hope I have a quick answer for you," said her attorney.

"What would happen if I were pregnant?"

"What do you mean, what would happen? None of the agreements would be valid. You can't get a divorce, if you're pregnant. Sherese level with me. I'm your attorney and if you're pregnant I need to know."

"Melanie, I'm not sure. I got sick after we left the courtroom, and I thought it was just a nervous stomach, then I got to thinking. I can't even remember when I had my last period. I think it could be just the stress of all of this."

"Sherese, you need to know for sure. Go to the doctor now. Call me as soon as you know."

Sherese said a prayer before she got out of the car at the Women's Clinic. The wait for the results was excruciating. The thoughts running through her mind were like little stabs at her heart. She couldn't afford a third child, but how would she be able to bring herself to abort this baby? She'd been excited at the news of Autumn and Anthony, but being a single mother of three would be too much for her to handle. And she knew she could never carry a baby, then give it away.

"Melanie, I just got the results back and I am pregnant ... almost four months."

"Damn, I was hoping it was a false alarm."

"Me, too. But, I took a home pregnancy test, then confirmed the results with my doctor."

"This news changes everything."

"What are my options?"

"We can re-file the divorce after the baby is born and paternity is established. Or you can terminate the pregnancy and no one will be the wiser. Thank God, we still have Roe vs. Wade."

"Why can't I get a divorce while pregnant?"

"The law was enacted to protect the rights of the unborn child. Supposedly, the divorce will make the child illegitimate. But, I just believe it is another attempt to give men power over women's bodies."

"I think I'd agree with that."

"What about adoption?"

"That is an option, but Steve would have to agree to give up all paternal rights before the child could be adopted."

"I don't think he'd do that. But he might, just to keep from paying child support for three children."

"Sherese, I can't help you make this decision, but I can tell you that ultimately you're going to have to do what is right for you, Autumn and Anthony. You can't let a group of cells that you don't even know affect your ability to raise the two children you already have. Take a couple of days to think about it and let me know what you plan to do."

Later, Sherese called her mother. "Mom, I've made my decision. Would you go with me to . . .?"

Tears dripped down Sherese's face. She had made a very difficult decision. Her mom embraced her and rocked her, soothing the lose hairs back into her ponytail. Maime wished she could take her daughter's pain away, but she knew she was helpless in this situation.

They arrived at the Women's Clinic to see a crowd of people holding signs. As they parked and walked toward the entrance the crowd began to scream, "Please don't murder your baby. Murderer! Baby Killer."

Sherese was shaking by the time she got inside the clinic. She thought, *No woman should ever have to make this decision.* The waiting room was full of women and girls who averted their eyes to keep from looking at anyone. There were several nervous looking men staring at the floor or at their hands. Sherese was just about to get up to leave when the door opened and a sweet-faced lady opened the door and called her code name. She got up slowly, pulling her mom up with her.

Inside the small room, they watched a short film that explained the procedure. Then they waited in another waiting room before they were called into the counseling room. The counselor said that she could change her mind if she wanted to. She talked about other options and agencies that could assist Sherese if she chose not to have the abortion.

Sherese confirmed her decision, signed all the procedural documents, and was sent to wait in the third waiting area until she could talk to the doctor.

The doctor explained the procedure again, and answered Sherese's questions. The procedure was quick and Sherese felt a strong sense of relief, mixed with sadness. She marked that moment as the lowest point of her life, but in her heart she knew she had done what she had to. She found a good counselor for her and her children. They were bonding as a family without Steve and she knew in her heart that she would make it work for their sakes.